SAVIOR UNIT

MARYELLEN HUNTER

ISBN: 978-1-7358448-3-1 (paperback)
ISBN: 978-1-7358448-2-4 (ebook)

DEDICATION

To all great patriots; know that a small group of people with the right talents can accomplish great things and set the world right.

..

THANK YOU

To my sister-in-law Annette who, once again, patiently slogged through my grammar and typos, while continuing to encourage my writing.

To Bob for continued assistance with editing and collaboration - we made it through another book!

To My beloved grandson Hunter, Brenda S, Patricia F, and Cathy RC my steadfast beta readers and cheerleaders!

To Lisa for realizing my writing was serious.

And to my son Marcus VI – still not letting me give up!

.

PROLOG

The population growth in the United States had placed an unsustainable burden on the economy. When a small group of aspiring oligarchs in top governmental positions viewed the declination of the economy, they shuddered at the possible risk to their plans.

Webster Dictionary defines Oligarchy as a small group of people having control of a country.

They had controlled the economy sufficiently to manage the dependent masses in a population being consumed by democratic socialism. As the barely sufficient government subsidies provided just enough social programs to control the needy population, their strategy had not taken into consideration how the open border policies would tip the scales toward a society of entitled. Funding for the programs was no longer available as the working class became the minority, limiting the ability of the federal economy to support the cost of the entitlements.

This group of oligarchs was known as the DComm Group, short for Decommission Group, whose plan to control the United States of America, had become hampered by a burgeoning population that needed to be thinned by a targeted reduction solution.

Webster Dictionary defines Decommission as complete withdrawal from service or use.

The DComm Group had attempted population control through incentive programs promoting and providing government paid sterilization and abortion. Though this plan cost the taxpayers billions of dollars, it didn't address the number of unhealthy or non-working adults currently inflating the population. The balance between the working class and their counterparts, the non-working and recipients of entitlement programs, was presently weighted heavily toward the entitled. This conclusion precipitated the need for a plan to eliminate unhealthy, non-working, non-taxpaying, and non-contributing citizens. They needed to initiate their insurance measure which they named Project Clearcut.

Webster Dictionary defines Clear-Cut as the removal of all trees in an area of forest. The term derived from the lumber industry which selectively removed large targeted areas of trees based on disease or lack of usefulness.

Project Clearcut was the planned distribution of a biological weapon on U.S. soil, to radically reduce large numbers of the population within select target groups while saving those contributors to the tax system and specific political voting blocks. The launch of Project Clearcut returned reports of extraordinary success. The number of deaths was staggering and the DComm Group was pleased.

There are some, however, who have discovered the

truth of Project Clearcut. This small team is committed to finding a way to stop Project Clearcut. Their goals are to save the population of the United States and remove the corruption existing in the present administration. They work undercover, sacrificing their freedom to collect the proof of the genocide and recruit an army of patriots intent upon educating the population on the plot of destruction against the nation, and ending Project Clearcut.

This group is growing, they are the SAVIOR UNIT...

PROJECT CLEARCUT

What information the Savior Unit had about Project Clearcut came mostly from Goose, the medical services android once assigned to the now-deceased Dr. Ellison Hampton. It was a miracle of sorts that Goose, formerly known as MSA121068, was even functional after its partial decommission. Fortunately for all, Joshua Klein and Beth McCallum had rescued and recommissioned it that it might complete its primary mission, 'Must Save Mankind'!

Through Goose, the Savior Unit had access to a wealth of information related to Project Clearcut including the Project Clearcut Mission statement and the location of the primary manufacturing facility.

PROJECT CLEARCUT
USA - DOD – TOP SECRET
8/14/2027

MISSION PURPOSE: The increase in the population of the United States of America has reached an unsustainable volume resulting in diminished land mass available for purposes of agricultural production. The ratio of working individuals to entitlement subscribers is weighted heavily toward the entitled recipients of government-provided resources.

As the population continues to grow, the USA usable agricultural land availability, and resulting reduced availability of viable food production is disproportionally diminished. The results of the associated statistics are considered by the government to have reached critical mass. The working-class tax dollars are insufficient to finance the purchase of food resources from other countries that still offer commodities for sale.

MISSION SOLUTION: Reduce large numbers of non-participating civilians in the USA.

The research model indicates the imminent need to reduce the population of non-contributing residents. The recommendation is to implement a targeted bio-medical solution, for which there is no cure, to quickly eliminate the drain on the country's resources. Analogous to the deactivation of an older model droid, we will refer to this necessary purging of non-contributing humans as Human Viral Decommissioning (HDV).

MISSION IMPLEMENTATION:

DOD and the US Army control the facility known as RiverMoore Laboratories. RiverMoore is a primary research and storage location of biological weaponry, virus, and bacterial research projects. RiverMoore laboratories will be commissioned to manufacture a biological weapon for the Army. Their security status will preclude them from the knowledge of the Primary Mission of this viral bio-weapon.

RiverMoore Laboratories will also be in charge of subcontracting the research and development of a vaccine intended for the list of intended protected governmental and designated civilians targeted for protection.

DOD will be a principal financier of the subcontracted vaccine research to ensure the security of the vaccine's limited distribution. Subcontractor lab (Security Against Virus in Outbreak Regions) SAVIOR LABS will, as with RiverMoore, be precluded from the knowledge of the intended distribution of the anti-viral vaccine and possible reagent.

SAVIOR LABS will be equipped with a state of the art MSA model android to assist in research with its primary goal being the maintenance of all records of research and development activity. This information will be automatically backed up remotely to data storage at the DOD Bearlywoke facility. MSA model droid will be custom designed and equipped with a nuclear power supply and GPS tracking capability until such time that it is decommissioned. DOD will also coordinate with the US Army for enhanced military defenses and assistance features built into the MSA model android for its protection.

IMPLEMENTATION TARGET GOAL: 6/14/2028
MISSION TARGET GOAL REACHED: 9/11/2029

The source of the bio-weapon, Bearlywoke Storage is owned and operated by the United States Department of Defense (DOD). Its function is to modify, package, and store for distribution the following four serums:

JMV2030 – The original bio-weapon with no changes to the name as it is the base product and not intended to be distributed to any facility other than SAVIOR Labs.

AVBW#Ds – Internally named version of JMV2030_R Randomized version of the original bio-weapon

AVBW#Gs – The AV_JMV2030 anti-virus to the bio-weapon (Government use only)

AVBW#Ss – An additional Bearlywoke product, which is a placebo.

A lower case 's' suffix indicates the newest batches of serum.

Bearlywoke Storage had been shipping large volumes of the AVBW# serums to other storage locations across the United States as the following list designates:

Los Angeles CA
San Francisco CA
Seattle WA
Houston TX
Baltimore MD
Minneapolis MN
Rochester NY
Buffalo NY
Philadelphia PA

Unbeknownst to the Savior Unit, quantities of the

JMV2030 (raw virus) and AV_JMV2030 (anti-virus) items had been shipped internationally to a Beijing, China laboratory before the launch of Project Clearcut within the U.S.

The JMV2030 is the only virus that is unmodified and stored at only two U.S. locations, Bearlywoke Storage and RiverMoore Laboratories (point of origin and manufacture). Small quantities of JMV2030 were transferred to the, now defunct, SAVIOR Labs for purposes of research and development of the randomizing agent and anti-virus products, but the remaining inventory was removed by Bearlywoke Storage shortly after the death of Dr. Hampton, former head of virology research.

TEAM BETH AND JOSH

Beth McCallum is Joshua Klein's best friend and cohort, with him through thick and thin. She hadn't changed her unruly red hair throughout their ordeal of being chased by the FBI across Texas as they attempted to protect the MSA121068 droid.

They had been identified as persons of interest in the murder of Dr. Ellison Hampton, the researcher who had developed the anti-virus to the deadly Human Viral Decommission (HVD) serum. Their goal during their flight, from the long arm of the law, was the protection of the decommissioned MSA droid, now referred to as "Goose". Goose held the proof of Project Clearcut and the oligarchy that was in the process of executing an undercover control of the government and was key to proving their innocence.

Beth's commitment to Joshua was unquestioned as was her determination to stop the Project Clearcut. They were both still being sought by the FBI for their suspected involvement in the murder of Dr. Hampton. For this reason, they continued their work while being hidden away, fighting the battles they could in cyberspace.

From the reports Josh and Beth had been gathering, it

appeared that a large portion of the police force was required to be the first to receive their vaccines. This was not in and of itself strange as essential persons are always first in line for critical therapies during any serious emergency. Studying this information, however, revealed that a high percentage of police had received or been designated to receive the #D serum. The question was – why?

They observed a sharp increase in violent crime which seemed to be a direct response to a radically diminished number of law enforcement officers. Outbreaks of violence occurred in lines of people waiting to receive the vaccines and mob riots against stores and homes were crimes of opportunity that criminals saw and capitalized on with this change in law enforcement presence.

Josh was a wizard of technology and had been Beth's idol and hero since college. He had been severely injured, at Savior Labs, in the process of retrieving the information needed to prove their innocence. Beth's medical background served to provide nurturing attention to Josh during his convalescence. He was now on the mend and their roles had been temporarily reversed even as he was still a magician with the computer, it was now her fingers on the keyboard performing the magic under his watchful eyes. She felt like the "Sorcerer's Apprentice" at times, but any time spent with Josh was a good time.

Both Joshua and Beth were currently undercover for their protection but they had more than their fair share of work to be done with the Savior Unit. They were fugitives from the law, but their labor was currently more important than proving their innocence. Their data searches were critically needed to build the charts and graphs for the creation of the target plans needed to recruit a civilian army across the country. Josh and Beth's work had the dual missions of saving the people of the United States and, through the exposure of the DComm Group, return control of the government to the people.

It was part of their jobs. within the Savior Unit, to track the relationship between the HVD deaths and the associated vaccinations received. There was a critical need for the collection of irrefutable evidence to prove that the viral epidemic sweeping across the country was not an unfortunate medical accident.

DELPHI

Chuck Delphi, Acting Director of the DOD, glances occasionally at his television – the sound is turned off, but it pleases him to see the images of the people waiting in lines to receive the vaccinations. The images showed misery, unlike nothing the United States had ever experienced. Worse than the breadlines, during the great depression, were the images of the country now.

People of all ages – in rain and shine suffering the lines, many angry, many sad, but the common denominator was the unmistakable look of fear. Fear of the HVD, the thing that could kill in just days with no warning, fear that the facilities will be closed for the night before they reached the door, fear that the facility would run out of vaccine before they reached the front of the line, but the greatest fear of all was the fear that they would be infected before they got the chance to get the vaccine that could save them.

The people had no idea what HVD meant, other than the fact it was killing people. They had no clue that the distribution of the HVD was a targeted plan to alter the population demographics and a plan to topple the American government.

11

Mr. Delphi delighted in seeing the fear on their faces because he knew the only way to ensure power was to control the masses with fear. The knowledge that he had the most fearful tool in the country was an elixir to his sadistic nature and his insatiable desire for power.

So he sat in his comfortable leather chair sipping on scotch, smiling at the images of desperation and suffering, thinking of the sexual marathon he would be having when he had another evening with Gracie Valentine.

She was his 'sexretary' and it made him laugh to think that she was easier to control in the bedroom than the many suffering on the streets. Soon, he will be leaving this place and it delighted him to think that she would also be on the streets with no other means to support herself. She had served his baser needs, but she was no spring chicken, and he fantasized about the possibility of her resorting to street prostitution once there was no longer a need for her talents in the comfy government offices.

The Clearcutting of the police force was, for the most part, necessary to ensure a valid reason to call up National Guard troops across the nation. Another way to control the people was to replace their protection from the rioting and looting with government-controlled law enforcement. The respect for the local law enforcement had been diminished as the DComm Group had chipped away at the structure of the government. The streets of the larger cities were portraits of anarchy. All television channels rolled video evidence of the fear that served to fuel the destruction and crime in every city.

The President was resisting the ordering of martial law. For a few weeks, the images had been pictures of people getting trampled during fights and riots. The other members of the DComm Group had, at last, prevailed upon her to push for the deployment of the National Guards in those states that were the hardest-hit areas of crime. She did one of her many press conferences to tell the people – the use of the National Guard was for their protection. Recently, the presence of the Guards' had affected some semblance of order but the lines of people waiting to get vaccinated grew steadily longer.

Chuck would have preferred if the President could be convinced to take that next step to martial law. He firmly believed that the individual State's Guards had a higher possibility of weak links, as opposed to a full out national police state. He could care less if the people on the streets were killing each other. His desire for martial law was to establish protection for the DComm Group, of which he was an integral part. The National Guards were limited to the use of water cannons, flash bombs, tear gas, and in worst-case scenarios, rubber bullets.

He would be delighted to see live rounds taking out large numbers of rioters and other troublemakers. In his opinion, if people needed to be contained, it should be permanent – the DComm Group power structure did not need insurrections. He recognized that there was a very fine line between civil disobedience and insurrection against the government. In the Chuck Delphi plan, civil disobedience was acceptable.

The most recent images and reports being shown on the television referred to a slight decline in numbers of makeshift tents and drug addicts, in many cases, laying in their waste on the sidewalks. This slight reduction was probably a result of the National Guard, who had taken up the order to begin transporting the homeless from their sanctuary cities to the free clinics and larger National Guard encampments that had been erected to house them until they received their vaccines. In some locations, the largest volumes of the populations' despicable had been transported by the truckload to get their vaccinations. This process was ordered by the DComm Group entities without the true defined reason for the action. The order was identified as a means to accelerate the number of vaccine recipients served, while in actuality the design was to facilitate the effectiveness of the Project Clearcut.

The cost of traditional medical care for recipients of the AVBW#D was significant for those who were fortunate enough to be treated in a hospital. But the virus worked fast, and the insurance programs were quick to capitalize on governmental subsidies to offset the cost of hospitalization and keep the sick moving quickly out to make way for replacement HVD sufferers. The hospitals were making fortunes on the epidemic.

Cities had to evaluate the cost of hospital care versus the cost of clearing the vermin in the streets. Some of the most heavily populated cities were faced with the continuous daily cost of waste cleanup and battling other diseases.

San Francisco, Los Angeles, New York City, Portland, and Seattle were overwhelmed with the battle against rodents and they had begun to suffer outbreaks of both bubonic and pneumonic plague in the homeless areas. The plague was not a fast-moving disease as the HVD virus, and this began to cost the cities in the treatment of the patients in addition to the difficulty in trying to eradicate the disease-carrying rodents.

Eventually, the larger cities used the now empty hotel rooms to house the many who were dying from the disease, all of whom had gotten their vaccinations, but unfortunately too late to save them from being infected (or so it was reported).

The DComm Group had determined that the National Guard camp solution was the best for dealing with the homeless populations. It would appear to be the most humane plan, by moving them to receive their vaccinations, the geographical relocations might reduce the vermin infestations of the cities. In the many National Guard encampments across the country, there were rows of tents erected to administer the vaccines in far less time than it took to process these homeless through medical facilities.

The millions of respirators that had been manufactured for the pandemic of 2020 were used in medical facilities across the nation. The videos of patients compassionately being cared for, while connected to ventilators and tubes of useless antibiotics, were good press images for the political campaign of incumbent President Talbot.

The National Guard tent cities did not have respirators. What the Guard tent cities had were the Guard's men and women trained to give the vaccinations, feed those who could or would eat, and do their best to keep the sick and dying as comfortable as possible despite the knowledge that there would be no recoveries from the HVD.

The Guard units were staffed around the clock, so the homeless were able to be vaccinated, then held awaiting transport back to their sanctuary city hovels. The news media was not privileged to see the numbers of recipients who didn't live long enough to be transferred back to their respective sanctuary city tents and makeshift sidewalk homes.

The question now was what to do with the bodies? Chuck Delphi would need to make a call to discuss a possible plan for this concern. The drug addicts and other homeless had no clue that they were going to their deaths by being transported to the National Guard camps to get the AVBW#D vaccine injections. When considering the lives they lived, Chuck saw their deaths as a service he was providing. to them. Most of these street people had been what many considered the 'living dead'. Chuck now pondered the possible disposition of the bodies.

PRESIDENT SANDRA H. TALBOT

The President was pleased to see the streets were being cleared of the vermin (both the two and four-legged variety), they were a drain on the economy and the two-legged ones didn't vote. In her opinion and that of the DComm Group, these people had no value. There were no training programs or psychological programs that would rehabilitate them. They were lower than ticks sucking the blood of the working people who kept the money flowing into the government coffers.

POTUS didn't want to seem insensitive but she was elected to run the country, not clean fecal material from public sidewalks. She had even wondered if it was possible to package a new serum using the raw JMV2030 and have it labeled as AVBW#HVD for distribution to those homeless collected up by the National Guard. She questioned the need for the delay that had been developed (the #R formula) and added to the original virus (to avert the discovery of the virus in use on offshore battlefields). A possible #HVD virus was a way to speed up the decommissioning process – with fewer dollars spent on frantic hospital attempts to save the doomed and useless lives. In her mind, she concluded that she would have to bring this question up in her next meeting with the DComm Group.

A drastic reduction in the numbers of these non-contributing citizens would effectively minimize the financial burden on the economy. As the incumbent president's bid for reelection was less than 10 months away, an improved economy equaled more votes. Her wife had said on numerous occasions that 'it seemed like the DComm Group didn't consider her bright enough to come up with ideas on how to run things. This was a great idea and they would have to give her credit for it!'

President Sandra Harrison Talbot has been at the head of Project Clearcut since before she was sworn into office for her first term. She'd like to think it was her idea – but she was nothing more than a single player within the DComm Group. Project Clearcut had been planned as a path to a much larger goal, the overthrow of the republic had begun more than a decade before.

The ecologic justice campaigners continued to march around believing that the change in the climate of the earth was related to meat-eaters and autos. POTUS and the DComm Group believed the real problems with the earth were the diseases that were spawned by a burgeoning population of welfare recipients, breeding, not working, and not getting vaccinated for diseases that had long ago been eradicated. The reduction in vaccinations naturally allowed these diseases and their mutations to return with a vengeance. In short, the overall health of the country was progressively weaker than in any previous historical era.

The homeless numbers were staggering as were the numbers of vermin and insects feeding on the waste in the streets of every major city in the nation. This pestilence brought a return of bubonic plague, an infection caused by a bacterium found mainly in rats and in the fleas that feed on them. People and other animals can get plague from rats or flea bites. In the past, the plague destroyed entire civilizations. The plague easily spread amongst the street people. The onslaught got worse as the rodents got bigger and bolder and their food sources were now openly present and abundant. And everywhere the rats traveled, they left their biting fleas and deadly bacteria.

For POTUS and the DComm Group, the death by plague was not fast enough, nor could it be targeted. To this group, targeted deaths were key to their control and success. In short, they needed a healthy working population.

DELPHI AND POTUS

Delphi detested the President – but she was part of the group, as such, he had to tolerate her until … well, such time that she was no longer needed. Chuck was partial to women who knew their gender and slept with men. But she was a dominant and fierce candidate and three years ago the people considered that to be a trait best suited to the ruling of a nation. He'd like to rape her – not because she was attractive, she wasn't, she had the boney body of a pre-teen boy. He'd like to defile her only for the reason that it would please him to control her as a woman should be controlled. It made him angry to think of her rolling around with a woman in the bedrooms of the White House, *yes* – he thinks, *I would love to rape and injure her in the process.*

He would make sure she was assassinated before the end of her term. The Vice President was a Mormon, Matthew Hominy, he couldn't do any damage in what would be left of her term, and he'd be easily replaced by a new person from the DComm Group power circle when his term was ended. *Perhaps, Stephanie Wolff,* he thought to himself, *she sure had the looks and the nerve, but she had no public name recognition. Oh well – maybe I just need to get my name more public and take the job myself.* But for now, he must continue to interface with POTUS so he places the call.

Delphi, "Madame President, how are you doing today? I know you are probably pretty busy with the elections less than ten months away now. But there is a delicate matter I needed to discuss with you."

POTUS, "Did you take time out of both of our very busy schedules to call me to remind me how busy I am? What do you need, Delphi, that is more important than my reelection campaign?"

Delphi, "Well we have an issue of what to do with the homeless bodies. As you know, we have been moving the homeless to remote tent city locations to receive their vaccines, and that they are dying before being able to be returned to the sanctuary cities of their previously known residences. They are, for the most part unidentifiable, with no next of kin to claim the bodies, so the question is what would you like done with them?"

POTUS, "What would you suggest, Delphi, mass graves, cremations, or is necrophilia one of your many depraved fetishes?"

Delphi, "No Madame President, I would not suggest any of those ideas, even the mainstream media wouldn't be able to keep a lid on something like that. I was thinking more along the lines of 'recycling'. And no, I do not have a thing about dead bodies, just trying to cover your ass, Madam President! Perhaps there are some pragmatic uses for the bodies. They could be used for medical schools (lab training), pet food, fertilizer, and macabre at it may seem, there are still soup kitchens feeding the remaining homeless."

Chuck knows that this egotistical bitch must believe that any good idea was hers. He has to drop some breadcrumbs to see if she can follow the trail to an idea.

POTUS, "Fertilizer then?"

Delphi, "Well, yes – for central plains areas – rural. And

East coast, the Ivy League schools could…."

POTUS, "Use the bodies for their medical students….And the west coast, Mr. Delphi. There are still too many homeless there – can the western bodies be recycled for the soup kitchens? And what about exporting the burger? I know that there are some Asian countries with limited protein sources due to the land consumption needed to support their burgeoning populations."

Delphi, "You are astute Madam President…." he thinks to himself - *as long as you follow a trail of breadcrumbs and hints.*

POTUS, "Make it happen, Delphi. And next time you need an idea – maybe you could put on your itty bitty thinking cap and spare me from doing your itty bitty job for you!"

Delphi thinks to himself, *nope couldn't rape her – couldn't get it up for that bitch!*

Unbeknownst to Delphi and POTUS, this conversation was recorded by his secretary, Gracie Valentine, and would soon be shared with the Savior Unit to be included in a growing dossier on the DComm Group.

NEWS MEDIA

The news media helicopters are circling the cities of Dallas and Fort Worth, Texas. The video's images are of lines – miles of lines of people in the burning heat of Texas near every hospital and medical center. These are lines, all waiting to get vaccinated. In addition to videotaping the lines, there are also scenes of fights, people being trampled in the fracas as the lines move painfully toward the approaching hour when the clinics will shut the doors for the evening or run out of vaccine. Everywhere are emergency vehicles, with first responders attending to the cuts and bruises and the many people who suffer heatstroke while waiting to receive the life-saving vaccinations. The city has stations with free bottles of water for the waiting, but it is too risky for someone to get out of line no matter how overheated they get.

Many of the fights were related to someone who left the line – to get water or food – but upon return, they were prevented from reclaiming their space in the line. The result was often physical violence because everyone in those lines lived with the same fear that the provider would run out of the vaccine before they got to the front of the line.

Every person suffered this fear in one form or another, but resorting to violence was common in varying degrees. The psychologists even generated a label, they called it "Territorial Possession Aggression Syndrome - TPAS".

There were 'experts' on talk shows giving 3-minute lectures to show hosts about the newly named TPAS, the excuse for the violence. The greedy psycho-babbling bottom feeders were delighted to have their prime real estate waiting rooms filled with court-ordered evaluations and treatment programs for recipients suffering from and convicted of perpetrating the street violence resulting from TPAS. It was just sad that professionals took advantage of the terror and was an example that no amount of window dressing will disguise a bottom feeder.

The videos were not scenes limited to the Dallas Fort Worth areas of Texas, the same insane behaviors were happening in every large city across the nation. The lines in the Northeast of the country were more desperate as they watched the clouds, heavy with snow or freezing rain, and listened to the weather forecasters' warnings about the coming winter season drawing ever more quickly to those areas. The Great Lakes region, with bone-chilling lake effect, promised to bring snow by the foot rather than the inch, which brought the line waiters to prayers that they might reach the front of the lines before the torrential fall rains or winter weather arrives. Minnesota, Wisconsin, and the Dakotas would soon reach sub-zero temperatures.

Those waiting in the central plains states prayed even harder for sufficient amounts of vaccines to be delivered to their cities. The rural central areas of the country didn't have the population numbers as many of those Great Lakes areas, but it seemed like the rural cities ran out of the vaccine much faster than the larger population hubs.

Some in the media speculated about what seemed to be fewer deaths per capita from this new epidemic, despite the vaccine shortages. Many farmers and regular blue-collar workers just kept on doing their jobs and didn't bother with rushing to get the vaccinations. They seemed not to be bothered so much about the HVD virus. Perhaps this was because there were fewer deaths in their states, or it could have been that they simply had more valuable work ethics and chose to do their jobs rather than stand in lines. Their goal was to feed the nation and they couldn't do it standing in a line.

The big city censuses contained volumes of welfare recipients leading to speculation that the disparity in rural deaths versus the city volumes was somehow nefarious in nature. The most conspiracy-minded people, who hinted that the lack of deaths could be related to the reduced number of vaccinations distributed in those areas, were targeted by the mainstream media for their suggestions.

There were those who hinted of a possible correlation between vaccinations and deaths suggesting the vaccines were the actual cause of the deaths. They were the ones with families or friends who died within days or weeks of receiving the vaccine, they were the ones suggesting the conspiracies. These stories were discredited by the mainstream and reported as reactionary to the personal tragedies rather than truth.

Joshua had been an avid researcher long before he went to college. The dark web was a sort of world of cyber-alchemy to someone with his hacking abilities. Now, this dark web was to be the encyclopedia of conspiracy for the Savior Unit. He searched long days and into the nights, wading through the noise searching for those threads that would lead him to clues. There were stories about the HVD deaths of people who had received vaccinations and links to the dark web contributors providing names of the hospital and medical worker whistleblowers. There were tales of employer demands to falsify records related to any possible suggestions of a correlation between the vaccine and death. Each of these threads became a superhighway for the wizard of the web and added to the data, which Beth was compiling into the Savior Unit dossier against the group referred to as the DComm Group.

The Savior Unit was monitoring the media and these stories closely. The conspiracy subscribers were the future Savior Army the ones who might be recruited to help target the media and hub distribution centers. They knew that they would need an army to defeat the DComm Group and Project Clearcut.

WANT ADS – LA TIMES

CLASSIFIEDS

LINE SITTER
$150/hr
Contact: 783-8872

WE SIT - YOU LIVE
Line sitter $150/hr
Contact: 563-1876

URGENT LINE SITTER
$100/hr Riverside
Contact: 658-5579

LINE HOLDING
$100/hr
Contact: Jim @ 477-6597

HEATED TENTS
Free delivery
Contact: 684-5597
Leave Message

STAY COOL TENTS
Free Delivery and setup
at your location
Contact: 477-6873

FIND YOUR LINE
Web for sitters
www.findurline fast or
Contact: 783-4685

**ARMED LINE SITTERS
SAVE LIVES**
$1800/day
Serious inquiries only
Contact: 477-8866 (Bubba)

The newspapers were overwhelmed in their want-ad sections now. The lists went on and on – more and more pages of want ads similar to the ones in the LA Times were consuming every major news platform.

There were 'line sitters' wanted and available, line sitter seekers, and line sitters willing to travel specific distances with per diem rates – references available upon request. Tax-free – some cash only – many accepting credit cards for a small extra service charge.

The media stories across the states were about people who were trampled or greatly injured and in some cases resultant deaths when the clinics ran out of serum. These stories spurred increased business opportunities to fill the needs of the frightened waiting for their vaccinations.

Tent cities sprung up around the blocks surrounding the clinics because if you lost your place in line, you were done for. Many entrepreneurs launched websites claiming that, for a small fee, you would be provided a list of target areas with recent deliveries of serum or shorter lines. They also offered, for a fee, a list of line sitters currently available for your desired location. And lest you need a little more for your money, these providers made available access to links for delivered food and beverages for your targeted area, of course, these links are also paid for by the food providers on a 'per order hit' basis. The food and beverage providers demanded enhanced prices to compensate for what they considered delivery to hazardous areas.

Diapers in sizes from infant through adult were delivered at extraordinary prices, not because of the delivery of the items but because the entrepreneurs had stockpiles of the precious items unavailable in the stores. All delivery agents carried some level of a weapon for self-defense, and the variety of weapons was diverse. There were pepper sprays, baseball sluggers, police batons, butcher knives, handguns, and in the roughest locations, rifles were seen.

Utility services were unreliable or non-existent as employees were afraid to go to work where they might be at risk of exposure to the virus. Unlike the 2020 pandemic, the government officials did not encourage the people to quarantine themselves, but rather encouraged the people to first get their vaccinations and then return to work to keep the economy solvent. The public services providers, however, were more afraid of exposure to the virus than being out of work – there were entitlement programs to subsidize their extended absences so the incentive to perform their jobs was diminished.

The reduced numbers of sanitation workers on the job contributed to the piles of trash and subsequent feeding and breeding of rodents. The increased presence of rodents brought with them the plague which was a far more miserable way to die, as it was not fast as HVD appeared to be. Many were hospitalized and misdiagnosed as having HVD when the true cause of their suffering was the pneumonic variety of the highly infectious plague.

Food shortages were rampant across the country as grocery stores became victims of vandalism, mob looting, or crash and dash robberies, while the limited police forces were unable to respond to the volume of crime.

Protection rackets popped up within these high-crime locations, and the people became victims of extortion and criminal behavior at every turn. The vaccination lines became opportunities for increased incidences of solicitation, drug trafficking, petty theft, and black market sales of comfort items from clothing to sleeping bags.

There were inflated prices for paper masks, hand sanitizer, and rubber gloves because the stores were empty of these now precious items. History repeats itself in all things and there were more examples of bottom feeders taking advantage of adversity.

DELPHI PROPOSITION

Joanna Moore's secretary, "Chuck Delphi calling, Miss Moore, do you want me to take a message?"

Joanna, "Thank you, no, I will take the call."

Joanna picks up the phone, "Mr. Delphi, I hope you are calling with some good news for a change."

Delphi, "Well I might say yes if you are missing my ruggedly handsome face....' (this remark elicited no response other than a pregnant silence from Joanna so he continued) Actually, I'm here in Fort Worth. I would like to meet with you to discuss a business proposition."

Joanna, "Business? I'm pretty busy with the RiverMoore business right now. I doubt if we would be able to consider any new ventures at this point."

Delphi, "The government, as you know has a lot on its plate right now that the RiverMoore bio-bug has gotten out – I believe that you are the only person qualified for this business proposal that I have. Look, I'm on my way to your facility, do you have anyone there who can make a pot of coffee? I had to fly commercial and I got peanuts and water and something resembling piss that they called coffee."

Joanna thinks, *Obviously he isn't the kind to take NO for an answer, so I'd better just see him and get it over with.*

Joanna, "Ok I'll have a pot waiting."

She'd love to put a dose of JMV2030 in his cup. It wasn't her facility that was distributing a deadly virus to the population it was under his direction that this was happening. This was the reason she was building the Savior Unit, to try to stop the damage he was trying to do by executing innocent citizens. He was part of a group that was perpetrating genocide and this needed to come to a screeching halt. But she knew this would need to be done with no loopholes for them to escape justice.

Joanna had decided before he arrived that she was not going to be run over by any conversation with the snake in the grass, Delphi. It's true, he is the Acting Director of the Department of Defense but that does not, in her opinion, cause a leopard to change its spots. She knows about their Project Clearcut and she knows he is in the thick of it.

Delphi didn't think very highly of Joanna Moore either. Her company, RiverMoore Laboratories was home to the world's most dangerous bacterium and viruses. This was the reason it had been selected to design and manufacture the bio-weapon, JMV2030. He didn't have high regard for any independent woman. *Of course, she named her creation JMV based, on her initials – An ego thing –* thinks Chuck.

The reported purpose of the viral weapon was to be an offshore military asset. To the best of Chuck's knowledge, she was never advised of the true purpose of the product. She was a scientist, first and foremost, the true intent for the JMV2030, to be used against U.S. citizens would have been a deal-breaker for Miss Petri-dish Moore.

The release of the virus into the population caught her unaware. This might be part of the reason he'd prefer her to be decommissioned. But at this time, he still needed her to manage Bearlywoke since the previous director, Doctor Yīshēng Swáng of Beijing, China disappeared from the

United States right at the beginning of the execution phase of Project Clearcut.

He knew where Doctor Y was but for optics he still had people trying to track Yīshēng down. Once Yīshēng had completed his mission in China, he would be easily apprehended and decommissioned. It would not be a gentle ending for the cowardly Doctor who had bailed on the DComm Group earlier than they had planned his exit to be.

Joanna had already requested her assistant to bring the tray of coffee with both cream and sugar options but advised her that he should not be served under any circumstances. As an afterthought, she tells her to make the coffee double strong, make sure it is tepid in temperature, bring paper cups, and find some of that dry powder stuff that pretends to be cream. It's not as good as a dose of JMV2030 but she hoped it would serve to annoy him since she couldn't kill him.

Joanna, "So, Mr. Delphi, what is your business proposal?"

Delphi, "Wow – that is direct Joanna…"

Joanna, "You may call me Miss Moore, thank you. I'm a very busy lady these days, please continue."

Delphi tries the room temperature coffee and is unable to suppress a bitter cringe, but said nothing as he tried to doctor the coffee with packet after packet of the disgusting white powder that refused to dissolve into the tepid sludge before him. He didn't notice that Miss Moore didn't indulge in the coffee herself. He thinks to himself, *if Gracie ever made coffee this bad she'd be out the door before she could pull her panties back on!*

Delphi, "Ok, we are all under a lot of pressure lately. To the point, Dr. Yīshēng has left the country. There is no indication of foul play that the FBI has been able to uncover. He sort of disappeared shortly after the virus got released, but finding him is our problem, not yours. The

CIA is investigating Dr. Yīshēng's disappearance. He is a foreign national, as such, he is not required to get permission to leave the country, it's just that his timing was awkward - leaving us without a location head. There will be no way of knowing if he was instrumental in the release of your bug until he is found and debriefed.... "

Joanna interrupted here, "Well I don't believe that I've ever met the Doctor. If I'm correct, you just stated that the missing doctor was NOT my concern, so please make your point for taking up my time!"

Delphi, "Normally, his assistant Terry Angel would be considered for assuming the temporary position of Acting Director, but she was a victim of a criminal act of violence which is currently under investigation."

Joanna, "Pardon me, a criminal act of violence? Related to the disappearance of the Doctor? I see that the FBI is looking for persons of interest regarding the death of Dr. Hampton, now you tell me you have yet another 'missing doctor' and criminal acts of violence associated with his assistant? It seems that the DOD is struggling with the management of their employees, so I don't understand why you are here in my office discussing your poorly managed human resource operations. RiverMoore is a scientific laboratory, not detectives-are-us."

Delphi, "Oh no – with regards to the assistant, my sources tell me it appears to have been an unfortunate but purely coincidental crime of passion.

It's a rather delicate matter from what I've been told.

What I'm left with, however, is an immediate need for an administrator to take over the directorship at Bearlywoke. The proposal I am making is that you, being the manufacturer of the virus, are probably best suited to take over the position. It is a very large facility and frankly, it is a national emergency that makes it necessary to continue its projects to provide the serum to stop the RiverMoore virus."

Joanna knows better – she knows exactly how Terry was killed – by a government-paid contractor named Art Damone who knows the truth about Project Clearcut and is now being protected by Joanna. Art Damone is one of her Savior Unit patriots working on the plan to save the country from what this Delphi monster is trying to do.

Delphi continued, "So to cut to the chase Jo… Miss Moore, we would like you to assume the Acting Directorship of Bearlywoke Storage until such time that a suitably qualified permanent director may be vetted and installed."

Joanna, "Well, you know I'm not a government employee, as such I am not qualified with the necessary Security Clearances, as evidenced in our last video conference meeting with the FBI…"

OUCH thinks Delphi – *petri dish carries a grudge…*

Delphi, "Jo……Miss Moore, you know you are the best qualified for the position, there is nobody else who knows the scope of the Bearlywoke project and its relationship to the RiverMoore virus. I can take care of the government clearances with a phone call – what else do you want?"

Joanna's assistant quietly entered with a china cup filled with perfectly brewed and delightfully aromatic coffee for her to enjoy in front of Delphi.

There it is again – his veiled suggestion that my company is responsible for the genocide that is happening - but aloud she says: "Balancing two companies, both involved in a national crisis, is going to take a lot of effort and resources at both places. I would need to have the ability to select and hire assistants for both facilities.

Considering that the virus was released from either SAVIOR Labs or Bearlywoke, I believe it would be crucial for me to have a hand-selected staff and the ability to define my own set of security measures to ensure no more mistakes are made. And I will need full access to SAVIOR Labs because, to date having no security clearance, I've had no access to the deceased Dr. Hampton's test records and progress results.

The PSA's indicate that the NSA is involved in the vaccination efforts. I would also need to select a supervisor within the NSA, in the medical monitoring area to have access to the continuing records of anti-virus distribution. Of course, I would select this person from the existing pool of personnel to ensure a smooth transition to the new supervisor who would be the interface between medical records and me."

Joanna continued with her demands: "Assuming that the JMV2030R bio-virus is still planned to be field-tested for military use, and considering that Bearlywoke has been performing the task of randomizing the virus, I believe that I could devise a plan to coordinate the process of military and civilian distribution of anti-virus serum.

After assessing Dr. Hampton's records, I can evaluate if the Bearlywoke facility could be dual purposed for the manufacturing of the military bio-weapon in addition to the increased production of anti-virus. Since there is a need for the anti-virus on US soil as well as offshore, the streamlined process of preparing and packaging the anti-virus at the Bearlywoke facility would provide the necessary security as well as serving the urgent needs of the U.S civilians.

This would allow the decommissioning of SAVIOR Labs leaving only one very secure facility (Bearlywoke) to be processing both the bio-weapon and the anti-virus. If I am correct, this was the original plan except for the increased need for anti-virus for domestic distribution."

This last demand was music to Delphi's ears! *She doesn't know that Bearlywoke has the manufacturing process working 24 by 7 already. The DOD had been satisfied months ago that the virus was going to do exactly what they had planned. And currently, she has no clue about the warehouse hubs containing the virus to be distributed as an anti-virus vaccine.*

One less organization involved in the manufacturing and

distribution process is in his opinion a GREAT idea. *This petri dish has some stones* he thinks to himself – *but she is organized and she still has no clue that Bearlywoke is Clearcutting the population.* He couldn't have planned for a better scenario.

Delphi, "Miss Moore I agree to your terms and requests and of course, you will be financially compensated for the elevated position. We need to book you a flight a.s.a.p. to Bluffdale, Utah where the NSA monitoring site is located. If you will email me a copy of your requirements for your employee coordinator, I can have Human Resources up there pre-screen prospective candidates and prepare a list of resumes and employee records that meet your criteria to streamline your interview process."

Joanna, "Ok Mr. Delphi, I will have that list this afternoon and I'll be expecting flight, transportation, and lodging reservations made for the day after tomorrow, and I only fly first class. More coffee, Mr. Delphi?"

Chuck Delphi had no idea that Joanna already had two NSA agents providing information about Project Clearcut. Beau Clark and Dave Tillis (NSA monitoring) had already become part of the Savior Unit.

Before all of this began Beau and Dave had been watching a game on TV, they had discussed the frantic monitoring exercises that had been going on over SAVIOR Labs. Dave, always ready for a good conspiracy challenge, spent some creative time – and was able to get information about Project Clearcut. The implications of what he discovered were not something to be pushed aside or ignored. The Project Clearcut mission statement named RiverMoore Labs, as the place the virus was made. When push came to shove, it only made sense for them to hack into RiverMoore to investigate which side of Project Clearcut the laboratory was aligned with. Dave was a hacker of the highest caliber and as well-acquainted with the dark web as Joshua Klein had been, but Dave Tillis had the advantage of being on the inside of NSA where – all things are known. Once they agreed that RiverMoore was not part of the project, he reached out to share the information they had acquired through their NSA monitoring. Dave and Beau had quickly agreed that Project Clearcut's mission was an assault on the entire population.

Joanna was pleased to share information with them because this gave her an avenue to monitor what the government was doing and who they were watching. The guys were more than happy to be 'secret agents'. They would soon be receiving their new titles and substantial financial improvements to do the things they would gladly have done for free.

TILLIS AND CLARK - PROMOTED

Dave Tillis and Beau Clark will, of course, also have that list of her requirements to tailor their resumes to be inserted in their respective personnel files. Joanna sent both Dave and Beau the keywords that were needed to ensure that HR included their names in the interview list. It was a quick job for Dave to update both resumes and enter them into the HR database. There had been no open posting for the positions. The HR person just ran a keyword search and printed out six resumes for each position to be interviewed. Miss Joanna Moore would be doing the interviews herself because the monitoring agent and analyst positions would be interfacing with her in Dallas.

Beau will be receiving a salary increase and dedicated upgrade to exclusive HVD tasks, which will give him more freedom to monitor data that will be of specific interest to both Joshua Klein and Beth McCallum.

Dave Tillis is an IT analyst with NSA. His position had been stagnant for years as it involved simple monitoring except for the most recent stuff. He was well respected for the many skills he possessed although most of his talent was wasted there. The pay was just ok. Secure jobs were not easy to find during this time of high unemployment in a highly competitive job market. This quantum leap was good for all aspects of his career including financial improvement, position status, and the ability to be a full-time cyber asset in the effort to topple Project Clearcut.

Beau Clark didn't have skillsets equivalent to his analyst friend Dave, but the position facilitated by Joanna, allowed him to be safely dedicated to the transfer of important data to Miss Moore. If he had remained a simple monitor agent, he wouldn't have had access to the critical data. The new title positioned him to be monitoring, under the Bearlywoke and RiverMoore umbrellas, and he received a handsome increase in salary as well.

Once these changes were made, Joanna was on the inside of Bearlywoke to work in concert with Cool Mann and some other "agents" he'd recruited in the lab and warehousing areas.

COOL MANN

Cool looks like someone out of a time machine with hair dreads disproportionate to his diminutive body. His arms and neck are covered with tattoos to coordinate with the tribal holes in his ears and piercings of his face. He had an attitude to match his weird presence, but everyone liked him despite the idiosyncrasies. His unusual look disguised his extraordinary skills of chaos control.

His clothing seemed to compliment his physical appearance. The large hibiscus floral Hawaiian shirts and surfer shorts seldom coordinated with each other in color or pattern. Often a pair of madras plaid shorts would be accompanied with a floral or bold striped shirt in sizes designed to fit a sumo wrestler rather than someone who was about 160 lbs. soaking wet. The ensemble always ended with his ageless Birkenstocks – Texas rain or shine, his feet were always flopping in his well-worn birks.

He had been well established in his career at Bearlywoke Storage in Highland Texas. He was thorough and innovative and a huge asset to both Bearlywoke and the Savior Unit. He didn't need to be recruited to join the Savior Unit. He'd been best friends with Terry Angel, the former assistant to the Director of Bearlywoke, and she had been murdered by a government-paid assassin. Her demise was a result of her attempt to help reveal the truth about the plans for the deadly virus. Sadly, her intent had cost her life.

Agent Adrian Mouse (FBI field agent) had contacted him about Terry and taken him to RiverMoore where he could be educated about the Project Clearcut and the true plan for the virus. He was not pleased to be told that he had been an unwitting party to the processing of the virus for several years. Of course, he was on board with the Savior Unit.

ADRIAN MOUSE

She misses Foote. Dave Foote had been her FBI field agent partner for over eight years. He had survived the blast of Goose's tools that day in the kitchen at SAVIOR Labs which must have been a higher current than what Damone had gotten. At this point, Foote was 'healthy', but just not sharp enough to risk involving him in a mission that could require fine perception and fast reactions. Her joining the Savior Unit was an easy choice after hearing Goose's story, and viewing the evidence, about Project Clearcut.

The department would be happy to assign her a new partner, but so far she had been able to decline, opting to continue her extended leave of absence. Getting a partner who is willing to go against the government that signs their paychecks wouldn't be easy. A new partner would need to be someone who has lost a family member to the virus – someone sharp – and very bitter...

Today she had contacted and made arrangements to meet with Travis Loki, assistant to Michael Carver Director of FBI. Travis's office is in Washington D.C., but he has been in Houston this week – burying his brother who died of a viral infection. Adrian drives across Texas to meet with Loki and offer her condolences, but mainly to discuss the DComm Group and possibly recruit Loki for the Savior Unit.

She had with her a set of photos as graphic reminders of the type of damage the virus had done to his brother and many others. She also has a copy of the Project Clearcut Mission statement and lists of the thousands of 'epidemic' deaths. When she presented the facts and photos she also told him that this list of warehouses must possibly be infiltrated or destroyed if humanity is to be saved - if his brother's death is to be avenged. She thought, *vengeance may be a bit dramatic, but in these desperate times, sometimes drama is the best calling card of truth.*

Mouse didn't know that Loki had already been doing some of the work that would aid the Savior Unit. He had been suspicious for months, but never dreamed that his family could be at risk. His decision to enlist the help of Gracie Valentine had been solely based on his suspicions about Darla Avery (CIA) and Chuck Delphi (DOD). The meeting with Travis Loki was fruitful in that they now had a Washington, D.C. ally.

GRACIE VALENTINE

Gracie was on the high side of her fifties but she worked hard at keeping her figure and looks under control with the use of cosmetic enhancements. Her sexual encounters were based mostly on how they could elevate her on the ladder of success in her career. Her constant suggestive gestures toward Chuck Delphi were nothing more than survival for her. Her sexual innuendos were, by design, not subtle. Delphi was, in her opinion, repugnance incarnate. But surrounded by younger women, she was compelled to use her sexual overtures to diminish her advancing years. She was a fine actress in the clinches too, so she continued up her ladder of success despite the disgust she felt when he touched her.

She wasn't a minority in the D.C. ladder climbers. 'Women's rights my ass' she said on more than one occasion during lunches with other D.C. secretaries from similar agencies. Her friend Angie Denzer would laugh whenever Gracie said that. Angie's boss was Travis Loki from over at FBI and he wasn't a lecherous dirtbag like Gracie's boss 'Dirty Delphi'.

Travis had recently mentioned the need for an escort to

attend a D.C. function and asked if she knew anyone outside of the FBI. Angie was happy to hook them up for a sort of blind date because she knew Mr. Loki was a nice guy who just needed to meet someone his age. According to Gracie, the date went very well and Mr. Loki was nice and a perfect gentleman. Gracie liked the idea of real dates with someone who wasn't using job security as a threat to have sex or move out of the way for the next candidate. She did have to be very careful in seeing Travis, however, because Delphi was a control freak.

She did what she needed to do with Dirty Delphi and spent some free time on discreet dates with Travis.

Travis began to speak in innuendos about something not right going on. It was stuff, he said, about some of those high-level players that were suspicious – suggestions there was something untoward related to that horrible virus. She had been happy to begin collecting and sharing some information with him. She would do anything if it was a means to a new manager who wasn't a horny piece of shit.

She felt really bad when Travis told her about his brother dying from the virus going around the country. Travis asked if she could find a way to take a little vacation with him. He told her he could use some help with making the funeral arrangements for his brother. Of course, she was eager for an opportunity to get away from Dirty Delphi for a brief vacation and she liked Travis.

Gracie invented a family emergency that required her presence in California (intent to keep her travel plans private). Dirty Delphi was happy to allow her to take off for a few days but suggested he'd sure be lonely without her. She knew what this meant, but it wouldn't be the first time she'd choked his chicken to get some small favor. *Small favor from a small man* she thinks to herself. It was amazing how she had come to loathe him. Chuck had said if she was going to be going through Texas, it was probably best for her to get vaccinated for her protection before she took off. He claimed to have heard rumors that there was an evil flu going around in Texas.

Well, she reminded him that she needed to go to California, not Texas, but Chuck reminded her that she would be connecting through Texas, so he strongly advised her to get her vaccination before traveling. He didn't want his best girl to get that horrible virus. Oh, Gracie hadn't considered the need for a connecting flight when she fabricated her trip narrative.

When she told Travis about getting the time off and vaccination, he asked the name of the vaccine she had received. She told him she thought the name of the stuff was AVBW#S. When she told him that, he sort of stopped breathing and said, "Are you sure it is #S, not #G?" "No," she had said, "I would have remembered if it was #G like Gracie."

As Gracie helped Travis with the arrangements needed in Texas, Travis mentioned that he had a meeting to attend with an FBI agent. He suggested that Gracie wouldn't need to attend if she would like to take a bit of time off. But she had been pleased to go along with him because, for Gracie, all things were about opportunities to advance Gracie's future. Her career had been spent climbing her way up the very competitive ladder of D.C. opportunities.

How fortunate for Adrian that Travis brought along a recruit so close to DOD. Gracie had been feeding info about Delphi to Loki for a couple of months now, but having her here in Texas, allowed Adrian to tell her how truly evil Delphi is. Mouse didn't know that Gracie was well aware of what a despicable being Dirty Delphi was.

Loki had been getting information from Gracie Valentine, about who was knowledgeable of Project Clearcut. When Gracie gave this information, she didn't know the Project Clearcut people would need to be exposed or killed to save the country. She only knew that her involvement might be a way out of working for Delphi.

During this meeting with Travis and Gracie, Adrian also tells the two of them about the multiple serums being dispensed. Gracie had a way of turning most conversations to be about herself and now she reiterated the fact that Delphi had made arrangements for her to get the #S vaccination.

It was time for Adrian to share important information with Gracie about the useless vaccine Delphi had arranged for her and how Delphi could still have her killed at will. Gracie was stunned to silence at this news. She was furious with Delphi, and now there is nothing she would not do to execute revenge against him. For Gracie, all things were 'about Gracie'. She became a full convert to the Savior Unit. Immediately after, she received a dose of the honest to goodness #G anti-virus vaccine.

At this meeting, Travis shared his knowledge of people in Darla Avery's (CIA group). He shared with Mouse and Gracie that Michael Carver had recently suggested to Darla Avery that someone might need to disappear. Then there was the Ackinsen car explosion just a day later. He knows Mrs. Avery is willing to kill for Project Clearcut, so the importance of secrecy is extreme. He reminded Gracie that though it is a good thing to keep her normal routine and contacts within D.C., she must never share her knowledge of the Savior Unit.

Adrian wanted to know if Travis had any idea why they would have killed someone who is part of that power group. Loki just said it could be as simple as reducing the size of the group, but their criteria for elimination could only be speculated at this point. They would, of course, share this info about Ackinsen with the Unit. It's all murder, but the targeting of someone so high on the food chain seemed to raise the bar.

Gracie agreed to continue feeding phone and communications information to Travis once she returned to D.C. It will please her greatly to be part of the effort to remove Delphi from his position of power. Mouse warned Gracie to be careful and keep close contact with the Savior Unit because she didn't have any protection in D.C.

Travis promised to keep close tabs and suggested that his secretary, Angie Denzer, and Gracie would both be able to stay under the radar, as they had been lunching together often for quite a long time. He also reminded Gracie that though it is good to keep the lunch routines with Angie, she must refrain from mentioning the Savior Unit. He also stated that he will find out if Angie had received the #G vaccine so Gracie shouldn't question this with her friend. Absolute secrecy must be maintained to protect all of their lives. Adrian shared with them that she had access to serum designation lists and she would check on Angie Denzer for them and make sure that Angie's designation would be #G. They all agreed that D.C. was not a place where secrets went unrevealed for very long.

SAVIOR UNIT MEETING

In attendance:

Joanna Moore
Joshua Klein (on video monitor)
Beth McCallum
Goose (MSA 121068)
Cool Mann
FBI agent Adrian Mouse
Art Damone

Joanna is heading up the meeting today being held in the basement of RiverMoore.

Joanna, "We are all happy to hear that your physical therapy is going well Joshua. We are going to need you in the trenches soon as you can put those magic fingers to the keyboard again. Miss Beth has been doing a great job here but she tells me that we are going to need a magician by the name of Josh."

She continued to share with the team the offer by Delphi for her to assume the Acting position of Director of Bearlywoke and the opportunities this will avail her to be on the inside of the packaging and distribution facility. This drew great applause and cheers, not because she needs another job to do but because they all realize the opportunities of having someone at the top of the food chain inside that House of Genocide.

Joanna, "We have been evaluating the target areas and possible solutions. What we've managed so far, thanks to our undercover Agent Cool", Joanna shifts her gaze to Cool and smiles, "is to have effected a change in labeling. The result is that the Bearlywoke warehouse is being filled with mislabeled AVBW#S. The #S serum is a placebo – but it is now labeled as AVBW#D. In other words, what we are doing is filling the warehouse with deceptively labeled harmless Cool Aid. Agent Cool, what are we doing with the bad stuff, the active killing virus?"

Cool, "Oh I got that covered, so far; the shift inventory people have a 'Cool list' that shows where they are to load from and instructions to be loading the older stuff to a van I have parked behind the warehouse building. It's a RiverMoore van, so when it drives out the guards assume it is a departing delivery truck. I rented a 'U Store It' space and the bad stuff is moving in there until you determine how to dispose of it. This rear loadout only happens during the graveyard shift and I've got the backside security camera on a video loop that shows nothing but cotton back there – no sign of that van sitting there or that it's getting loaded. I had to give the anti-viral serum doses to a few of these people and their families for their protection and allegiance to the cause of saving the world. I have enlisted some warehouse forklift operators to ensure that they only load outbound trucks with our special Cool Aid.

I also took the liberty of making a slight change in labeling. I considered a color change but couldn't risk some 40-watt warehouse worker noticing, so I added a lowercase 's' at the end of the serum name. It is almost equal to a typo, but it's programmed. If anyone questions it – I'd say 's' is for September. When we start trying to isolate the stuff that already made it to the USA hub distribution centers, we will be able to see the bad stuff, by the absence of the subletter suffix. I could change it every month, to avoid suspicion, if you think we need to do that. ANY suffix character will identify it as Cool Aid." Cool chuckled at his own joke.

Joanna, "Great job Agent Cool. The next item we need to discuss is how we are going to be purging the hub locations. Do you have a list of the distribution centers for me?"

Cool, "Far as I've been able to tell, they are only Los Angeles, San Francisco, Houston, Baltimore, Minneapolis, Rochester, Buffalo, and Philly."

Joanna continues, "This week I will be hiring Dave Tillis and Beau Clark in NSA monitoring to new positions where they will be monitoring mortalities. What we should see is declining numbers of deaths due to the virus as our Cool Aid is replacing the #D vaccine."

Mouse, "It's gonna take special ops to commandeer that many warehouses. It will have to be well-coordinated to be done simultaneously - something to look like a terrorist attack if we are going to just destroy the distribution centers. I know a guy who knows a guy, a patriot, who has the tools and background to make it happen, but I'm not quite ready to broach the subject yet. I don't have the contacts to access 'for-hire dark ops'. If we can put this together, there will be collateral damage, but we can try to make sure it happens on a weekend to minimize that." The guy who knows a guy – is Loki – the assistant to Carver FBI, who knows Darla Avery & CIA staff.

Joanna, "So how do we recruit teams to take these facilities down? I agree that it would have to be a well-coordinated mission. If we try to hop-scotch the country, the DComm Group will notice and tighten security on all remaining hub locations. PLUS Bearlywoke could come under scrutiny."

Mouse, "If we have to go that route to physically take down the hub warehouses, it will take a larger army than we have here and it will need to be flawlessly planned and executed very efficiently. One mistake and the only team in the country with a snowball chance in hell of stopping the genocide is done for."

Joanna, "I expect that by the end of this week we will be getting data from NSA about fatality numbers and locations so we can do better targeting – Josh and Beth will be tasked with the processing of this data. And though it is a sore spot with you, Mouse, we do have Art Damone who sure has tools. I think we need to give him a chance to at least bring some skin to the game." Joanna squinted her eyes causing a deep furrow to appear on her otherwise unblemished forehead as she continued, "Don't give me that look Mouse, you know he believed he was saving the country – he thought that Goose was in foreign hands, he didn't know the virus was intended for use on Americans. I think if I could cuff both of you together in a room, and you could hear how he feels about what we are trying to do, you might change your mind about him. He was misinformed. I believe that if you would listen to him, you'd see he deserved some redemption."

Art sat quietly thinking, *best I keep my yapper shut for now.* He did have tools beyond the elimination of soft and hard targets – one of which was to know when not to interject his opinions.

Josh from a video monitor, "I haven't had what I consider to be a safe link from here, so I've been monitoring television reporting and talk radio about the outside world and I've been collecting up a list of media people. I need better access into the dark web, Joanna that is where I'm going to find what we need. Not the mainstream bunch of liars – but the ones who are suggesting conspiracies – saying for instance that– in the heartland of the country, they aren't getting much distribution of the vaccine, and even the ones who are getting it, aren't dying. These media people are discredited by the mainstream, but we know this is not a conspiracy – these people are the breadbasket of the country and the Fort Knox of international trade. There is a reason they are being saved with or without our Cool Aid. Some of these conspiracy theorists may be suitable for recruitment by the Savior Unit. Once I get to a place where I can access NSA medical website records, I will be able to cross-reference the vaccination designations for these heartland cities."

Joanna, "Well I'm working on that Josh, as I said earlier within a week I should have two assets inside NSA one in monitoring and one in charge of the medical database, so we should be getting that information for you. And keep up that list of the media conspiracy journalists – that sounds like a possible opportunity for both virus data correlation and recruitment."

"Will do", said Josh.

Joanna, "I have a few ideas to bounce off Emmett Rankin about PSA's. Are there any questions? If not let's get back to work. We will be back here on Saturday at 9:00 PM."

RANKIN

Rankin (CDC) had been providing continuously looped file footage and false reports of deaths to ensure that people would keep coming to get the actual anti-virus. There was a downside to employing this false narrative. The increasing number of injuries resulting from people desperate to be vaccinated before the serum runs out was problematic. Unfortunately, this was a risk that was outweighed by the greater good of getting the people vaccinated.

The virus was not airborne, Rankin and the Savior Unit knew this – but the people didn't. The models had shown that there was less than .00001 percent chance of infection from physical exposure to an infected person. The public, however, would never be convinced of this fact because they had the President of the United States promoting fear of HVD.

Joanna had her RiverMoore people doing extensive testing on the Bearlywoke modified virus. Her concern was the possibility of the virus mutating. Being that the virus was a Corona based culture it could, naturally or artificially, be altered. This was critical knowledge and another reason why she wanted to ensure that they designed an actual functional anti-virus serum.

If Rankin went against the President with the truth, he would be stripped of his position and replaced with someone who would issue more lies to support her campaign of fear. These facts had been discussed with the Savior Unit and it was unanimously agreed that the best path to success was to protect the people by providing what they demanded (a true vaccine) until such time that the Savior Unit was able to provide the truth to the public. This truth would destroy the DComm Group, only if the Savior Unit was able to build an undeniable and overwhelming proof of the Project Clearcut.

He did express his concern with Joanna regarding the possible discovery of the conflict between his looped file footage and any live video footage reported on the news media. He needed people to get those vaccinations, but he needs a way to calm people and reduce the rioting. The injuries from the desire to get the virus weren't great news in Rankin's opinion. *Well* thinks Rankin *injuries aren't great, but better than receiving a #D vaccine and sure death.*

Next week he will be meeting with Delphi and that group, as Director of CDC, it is the only thing he can do. He was currently working on a possible solution to quell the rioting. They couldn't risk debating this, as it would be an admission of the DComm Group's desire for the continuation of the rioting and killing. He would have them over a barrel on this point.

Anything outside the realm of media contribution could raise questions. Delphi had made it very clear that Mr. Rankin had a very limited role – that of data reporting as it related to the viral death statistics and getting the people to the facilities for their vaccines.

Rankin's continued communication with the Savior Unit was providing very valuable information used to assemble the dossier that would be the weapon used to take down the DComm Group.

JOANNA AND RANKIN

Joanna, "Mr. Rankin, as the Savior Unit has been infiltrating the storage locations and swapping out the HVD active virus, we are seeing fewer people dying and smaller lines waiting to receive a vaccine. I'm sure I don't need to express the possible repercussions if this fact comes to the attention of the DComm Group. So what can we do to prevent this from happening?"

Rankin, "Well Miss Moore that has also been on my mind. I came up with a few ideas to bounce off you."

Joanna, "Bounce away, Emmett."

Rankin, "My first thought was to run loops of the older video showing the large numbers of people. I have been doing this already. There is plenty of media footage that I have been employing to make this happen. But knowing that the NSA is monitoring everything, someone with too much time on their hands could pick up the duplication of cities. There is a possibility of current local media footage conflicting with my older images continuously being looped.

I also thought of a PSA with a false video showing healthy survivors, though I'm not sure this would stop the

61

rioting. Next, I considered a new series of PSA's to encourage people to 'schedule appointments' for vaccines. This would get people off the streets so media coverage would naturally show the lines disappearing without alarming the DComm Group."

Joanna, "Well I agree the healthy survivors might send a signal that people are getting saved by our Cool Aid, as we are building substantial inventories of actual anti-virus. We need the people to get their injections but not at the risk of the hordes and rioting to make it happen.

I like the last idea of encouraging scheduled appointments to get the vaccine. Could the new PSA video indicate that scheduling appointments would decrease the existing problem of clinics running out of serum? That for instance, clinics and doctors would be able to better anticipate their serum needs based on the appointment schedules. If the people were presented with the assurance that they would be getting their immunizations without standing in lines, it might encourage them. One of their largest fears came from the clinics running out of serum. If our message focused on the reduced chance of clinics running out of the correct serum, this might give them more confidence in the new process."

Rankin, "Yes Miss Moore, that would be, in my opinion, the best path forward to get the people off the streets."

Joanna, "OK Emmett – that sounds like a plan – you probably need to propose it to Delphi – he and I have a rather contentious relationship. And since I'm juggling Bearlywoke with RiverMoore, I can't risk setting his alarm bells ringing. In the coming week, I will have assets inside the NSA with access to death statistics if you need that information. We can have NSA set up a secure link for you to access the information remotely to ensure your risk of discovery is low.

The next item I need to discuss with you is a much bigger project. At some point, the virus will no longer be a concern. The next step in our Savior project is to cut off the head of the snake, as it were. We will soon be planning a rebellion to regain control of our government. What we are going to need is an underground campaign to promote and organize the resistance. There will be no need for political correctness on this venture. We must get the divided country to come together to regain what is being taken from us."

Rankin, "Miss Moore, I will start immediately on the PSA stuff and perhaps brainstorming the rebellion idea. But you know no campaign can come from the CDC. The DComm Group is capable of cold-blooded murder. It wouldn't bother me to lose my job at CDC, once I have no value from inside the government, but I'm not wild about the idea of being assassinated. I believe that I can develop a strategy but someone else (not in D.C.) will need to execute it."

Joanna, "None of us want that Mr. Rankin. Let's hope that we can oust the DComm Group and you will be able to get back to your normal work with the CDC."

PSA

Emmett Rankin steps to the podium, the cameras are ready to film the video. "My fellow Americans, I am Doctor Emmett Rankin, Director of the Centers for Disease Control and Prevention. We have been observing across America, the level of crimes perpetrated, in reaction to the current epidemic of the HVD virus. As winter approaches our country, we have been evaluating the concern about people standing in lines during inclement weather in addition to the rampant violence. We understand the reason for the lines at the medical facilities, and the CDC is concerned equally about the medical well-being in addition to the safety of all American citizens.

We have had a panel working on the plans to launch a solution to respond to this street violence as well as looming environmental concerns as winter approaches the country.

There have been reports of black market vaccines that are not controlled, tested, or evaluated by the CDC nor the FDA. We have acquired sufficient quantities of these off-market vaccines and our test results indicate a range of responses from useless to lethal in laboratory animals.

As a result of the testing, we would like to stress the importance of getting the vaccine ONLY from authorized medical facilities and to avoid and report to the CDC or your local authorities, any offers of medication from non-authorized providers. At the end of this presentation, we will provide contact information for civilian reporting of these illegal and dangerous offerings.

Returning to the task of providing valid inoculations; we will be implementing a policy that will provide vaccinations by appointment only. This measure is to ensure the medical safety of all the citizens while deterring the criminal behavior that has been dangerous to those attempting to get vaccinated. What we've seen across the country in chaos are people wishing to be protected from the deadly epidemic.

The CDC has been working in coordination with the White House, National Security Administration, and the State's National Guard on the development of a plan to safely solve these concerns. Beginning tomorrow at 9:00 AM Eastern Standard Time, the offices of the CDC will have a new website available for all citizens who wish to get immunizations against the HVD virus epidemic.

Medical clinics, hospitals, and doctor's offices have been advised that vaccinations must be administered only by appointment. This will alleviate the crowding and shortages of vaccines, as the appointment process will allow providers to more efficiently order the needed vaccines.

We have enlisted the assistance of the Army National Guard in all states to set up temporary locations to administer vaccines as a supplemental solution to medical facilities. They, unlike medical clinics, will be staffed around the clock with personnel who are trained to administer the vaccinations.

The Website, www.HVDappointment.gov will provide listings of your nearest National Guard location and allow you to pre-schedule your vaccinations using an appointment tool in the program. The appointment tool will allow you to select a local medical provider or a National Guard location closest to your zip code.

If you do not have transportation to your nearest National Guard location, you may click on the box in the appointment schedule form to receive military busing information.

Libraries and public service offices have computers and assistance for scheduling your appointments. If you do not have internet access, you may call 1800 APPOINT. If you attempt to contact your medical provider directly, you will encounter further delays, as your service providers are also required to go to the scheduling process through this same web portal, to ensure that you get the proper vaccine. The fastest way to schedule your appointments will be through the website which will offer a list of language options for non-English speaking requests.

The website will provide the means to pick your nearest city and state to return a list of local non-military providers and their phone numbers to schedule your appointment for those cases where there is not a military facility in your area. All medical and military facilities are requiring appointments. The appointment process is critical to avoid unnecessary long lines and subsequent criminal activity.

We cannot, strongly enough, stress the importance of only getting vaccinated by authorized providers. For your safety and fastest possible service, we encourage you to use the appointment protocol to get your vaccinations through approved locations,. If we can all adhere to the new scheduling policy, we will be able to protect more people in less time.

This public service announcement will be repeated at the top of each hour on all television and radio stations. Thank you and God Save America."

Chuck Delphi was not pleased about this announcement. He didn't care if people died from counterfeit vaccines or mayhem in the streets. These were in his opinion, collateral damage. But Stephanie had no concerns and it was, after all, her domain that had to process all those appointments. He decided it was best to say nothing.

LOKI RECRUITS ROCKWELL

Travis Loki (FBI – Carver's assistant), who is now part of the Savior Unit, must meet with General Rockwell to show him the Project Clearcut mission statement and get him on board with the team. It's a risk, he realizes, to try to recruit a multi-star general to go against his President, but he also knows that the Savior Unit needs much more backing than a handful of civilians to take on the power group.

He takes his SD containing the current compilation of military and government employee medical targeting lists. It is his fervent hope that these lists coupled with the Project Clearcut mission statement are the tools Loki needs to bring General Allen Rockwell into the group. He knows that the General is not part of the DComm Group because of the incident that happened in the FBI meeting between Carver and the General. It had been an ugly scene between the two of them because Rockwell was clearly out of the loop with regards to the true intent of the virus plan. It was obvious that the General was outside the circle of trust and he was pissed off about it. He'd been dismissed from the meeting for plausible deniability reasons and to Loki's knowledge, Rockwell had not been invited to any subsequent meetings. Loki does not doubt that he will soon have the Army at their back.

JOANNA AND DAMONE
INFILTRATE STORAGE PLAN

Joanna thinking, *If we could infiltrate the nine distribution centers to place orders for known packages of #D and #G without subscripts by ordering thru the NSA med site, then the Savior Unit teams could pick up orders of the bad stuff and drop them at rental storage locations. Nothing would be left but Cool Aid or genuine #G serum in those locations. This seems right up Art's alley. He's got the tools and background to become a pickup agent – it's only nine locations. This concept wouldn't involve possible collateral damage from explosions.*

Joanna, "Art we have a conundrum with these hub distribution centers. I know you are in the habit of having a creative license to handle your projects in your way. But I honestly feel like nine national hub locations might not be the best task for a single person. So what I'd like to ask is, how do you feel your talents are best served in this mission we have before us? I sort of made a list of action items, but I'd like to hear what you have in your head on these things."

Art, "Well I've been thinking a lot about these matters

71

and you are right, this project does need a team. It's bugging me about the Chinese doctor disappearing right after he had me dispatch his assistant Terry Angel. He had no reason to disappear from the USA and this doesn't sit well with me. Have you found anything out about his whereabouts yet? I know your focus is on saving the USA and I am in total agreement with that, but the disappearing Dr. Y, that is just a burr under my saddle – I don't like loose ends. So whenever we get these hubs taken down, I think I need to find what he's up to and fix that up too. But that's just a personal mission for my head if you know what I mean."

Joanna, "I get that, about Dr. Yīshēng, but that is the lowest priority – agreed?"

Art, "Agreed."

Joanna, "So continuing to the USA distribution centers: We have nine hubs – some still contain the originally labeled serum – the bad stuff that we need to find a way to remove and destroy. I don't think we can safely get someone on the inside to work undercover to do this because it is my understanding that there are several hundred working three shifts doing warehousing functions."

Art, "Okay. Someone has to send an order to the hub to get some amounts of serum delivered to their hospital or clinic, right?"

Joanna, "Right."

Art, "We have the US Army at our backs, right? Why can't we simply fabricate orders for #D and #G and have the Army pick them up and transport them to armories and storage warehouses until you determine the best way to dispose of the bad stuff. That way if we need #G, we have it."

Joanna, "So we just need to put the Army on the transport task and Beth to building military-looking asset orders. But Art, does the National Guard have warehouses in any decent proximity to the hub warehouses?"

Art, "Holy shit, Joanna! Every major city has a National Guard armory within a few hours' drive! Their warehouses probably aren't refrigerated though."

Joanna, "The active virus is best kept cold, but we are just going to destroy it anyway. It's probably best if we leave the #G in the hub storage units – that way they will be kept cold until we can do a major move to the final destinations."

Art, "Who's going to get the Army on this?"

Joanna, "I'll contact General Rockwell about the pickups. Can you start working on a plan to recover bad serum that has been distributed to the medical locations? Work with Josh and Dave Tillis on getting you inventory lists and locations then we will discuss how to recall and collect that, ok?"

Art, "Ok I'm on it. I'll call Dave and Josh soon as I get back to my space."

Joanna messages General Rockwell that the Savior Unit will be needed to move assets, details to be provided in forty-eight hours. Rockwell designates Sgt. Wright to contact General Yabo with the request to prepare the National Guard warehouse space and security at locations near the nine hub cities.

Beth researches Government purchase order forms and recreates them for their special orders. Quick print operations are everywhere in the USA, so cases of false order forms were shipped to the list of National Guard locations. Sergeant Wright was the Army coordinator authorizing the orders of AVBW#D and #G from each of the nine city hubs. The orders were designated to be 'picked up by' not 'delivered to'. The distribution centers would not question the increased volumes of purchase by the military because they had seen the reports indicating that the Army was setting up inoculation centers across the USA.

TILLIS – NSA REPORTING

Dave Tillis was thriving in his new position as a supervisor in the Medical Records section up in Bluffdale, Utah - NSA monitoring. He had recently filtered his search to list alphabetically all government employees, by agency, followed by vaccine type ordered. Of course, the list was long – but the last filter, by vaccine type, let him show those at risk. He had added a field to separate the deceased to a separate list. This information was received by Goose remotely as Joshua had collaborated with Dave in the programming similar to that done by Dr. Hampton. Goose was a full-time recipient of all Tillis endeavors. Dave knew this but it was planned – and far more secure for both he and the Savior Unit.

Goose sent the recent search data to Joshua who was then able to generate recruitment lists. They knew that the more government entities recruited, the greater their chances of further infiltration within the government. Joshua's compiled list was conveyed to existing Savior Unit entities in D.C. knowing that these lists are a powerful tool in the recruitment process. When someone sees their name identified on the list to be decommissioned, it is a pretty profound incentive to join the fight.

Joshua's was a comprehensive national list to access in case a possible recruit wanted further verification of family or friends' status. The national listing was too large to be shared in its entirety, but he and Beth had access to very robust equipment, so individual requests could be executed quickly.

FBI - DOD - ARMY MEETING

Criminal related deaths continued to rise in proportion to the reduced police presence, so Delphi and Carver collaborated on how to implement martial law and the imposition of strict curfews. The Project Clearcut goal was to reduce the population, but they didn't want to risk an anti-government revolution, they only wanted select population groups to be eliminated. Riots and mob violence were not targeted deaths. Mob violence could risk the loss of functional working citizens and the DComm Group didn't want that to happen. The group desired to control the people and they wanted martial law nationwide. They would have liked to get General Rockwell to act on the National Guard deployment but, by law, the National Guard is called upon by the individual states. Sadly, the thing they wanted most would need to be ordered by the President, as she was the only person with the authority to declare martial law.

Location: FBI meeting room

Michael Carver (Director FBI)
Chuck Delphi (Acting Director DOD)
General Allen Rockwell (US Army) on teleconference –
sitting next to him - Staff Sgt. James Wright

Carver, "General Rockwell I'm here with Chuck Delphi DOD – on secure speaker. Can you hear me?"

Rockwell, "Yes Sir, I can hear just fine. My regrets I couldn't do the video conference, we've lost many good people from the damn virus, Sir. Some of them were techies – so we are limping along, as we try to get replacements trained to do the jobs of the lost, Sir."

Carver, "Understood. We have some concerns about severe street violence across the nation as it relates to the reduction in the number of law enforcement. The diminished numbers of boys in blue have had a crippling effect on controlling crime. Like the military, it takes time to adequately train replacements, so what we have is a real shortage of assets to control things in the cities. We've seen some improvement where the National Guard has been deployed. So what Delphi and I were thinking was perhaps the best way to go at this is to deploy the Army – to a state of martial law to get things under control."

Rockwell looks at Sgt. Wright and points to his ears to receive a thumbs up indicating that he is hearing this recorded meeting very clearly on his headphones. With the thumbs up from Wright, Rockwell proceeds with his conversation. "Well Sir, if that is your intent, you dialed the wrong person to this meeting because...."

Carver interrupted, "YOU are a three-star general and you can do any fucking thing you want with your army...."

Rockwell, "Sir, what I CAN do is order National Guard deployment in the states that are declared to be in states of emergency by the governors of those states. I do NOT have the power of a national declaration of martial law which seems to be the thing you are suggesting, if I understand your position correctly, SIR."

Now Delphi jumps into the conversation. "Let's be logical here gentlemen. General, we are not suggesting you break any laws, we are saying that because the law enforcement has lost so many assets, the military must protect the country from the domestic lawlessness we are currently seeing. We are suggesting a temporary nationwide solution to put things in a less dangerous environment for those citizens just trying to get the life-saving vaccine."

Rockwell, "Sirs, assuming that I am addressing both Mr. Carver and Mr. Delphi, at the risk of repeating myself, I state for the record that the National Guard is called upon by the governors of the individual states in the event of a declared emergency. The governors would contact me and I could order the deployment of the individual states' Guards. Period – that is my job, Sirs."

Carver was so angry, he looked like his head was going to blow up, "Are you saying that you refuse to act on an order from the DOD, General Rockwell?"

Rockwell, "Sirs, I do not take orders from an ACTING DIRECTOR or Director, sirs. What you are suggesting is that I circumvent the lawful protocol to initiate martial law. The martial law act must be ordered by the President of the United States and from what I know about martial law is that presently there is no legal reason to enact this radical action, and I have not gotten a call from POTUS to indicate otherwise, Sirs."

Delphi, "You are dismissed, General, and you might be advised to get your resume updated and your vaccina..."

Rockwell disconnects the call while Delphi was in mid-sentence, 'Wright, did you get all of that?"

Wright, "Yes sir – I sure did. Sir'

Rockwell, "Good man, Jim. I think it is time to take charge of what is left of this government. You can bet your ass they will be on the phone with POTUS before the end of the day.

Please call Josh K and tell him I need to conference with him to coordinate the breach of nine distribution hubs and coordinate the AVBW#G anti-virus for all armed service."

Wright, "10 4 Sir."

Bearlywoke has shipped millions of units of viable AVBW#G to armed forces bases across the country – it is waiting to be dispensed. This is no Cool Aid – it is the true anti-virus protection.

ROCKWELL
AND
DREW LEGEND - DHS

Rockwell was not pleased with the direction that Delphi and Carver seemed to be going. He understands the use of the Army National Guard and there were currently less than a dozen states that have sufficient incidences of riot-related crime and subsequent viral-related criminal deaths to qualify the employment of the National Guard. In his opinion, these issues could be handled by the local police with the assistance of the local National Guard, not full deployment.

With the National Guard backing the police, normal riot control can include non-lethal measures to dissuade the masses from aggressive behavior. Martial law is a whole different scenario. In the case of martial law, the Army doesn't use water guns, tear gas, or flashbangs to disperse crowds, their orders are to employ deadly force without hesitation when confronted. He was pretty sure that Delphi and Carver know this difference. He suspects that their insistence upon the implementation of martial law seems like they have a much larger plan than the control of isolated rioting.

The information from Loki confirmed that this power group, of which he was not a part, is best described as domestic terrorism.

Rockwell is a General, as such, he knows how to follow orders to the letter, but he is also a human being with a conscience and a loyalty to protect the citizens of the country against terrorism both foreign and domestic. He was extremely conflicted right now and he knows that the only decision he can make will be to defy orders from his commander in chief.

Rockwell calls his Staff Sgt. Wright, "See what you can find on Drew Legend for me ok? I need to know what side he's on with the administration."

Wright, "Sir, you mean his party affiliation 'side', Sir?"

Rockwell, "No, as in, can I trust him? Remember the thing about the virus, the Army was outside the circle of trust. I need to know if Legend is outside or inside of that circle. And this needs to be personal and secure – got it?"

Wright, "Always Sir, you need this yesterday?"

Rockwell, "As always....Jim. And Jim, we may soon be at crossroads when defying a POTUS order, an act of treason may be needed to protect the country. I need to know if you can be with me on this. If you can't, I understand and would ask that you request a transfer to save yourself from conspiracy to commit treason. I have relied on you and respected your loyalty and commitment for quite a while Jim, but I would never order you to be implicated if you disagreed with what I believe may need to be done."

Wright, "Sir, I swore the oath to defend the United States against all enemies, foreign and domestic. The other part about following the orders of the President, well that oath was written based on the President's compliance with her oath of office. The way I see it, the constitution has no provision for POTUS to commit genocide against her own country. My second in command has been you, sir. Considering that the commander in chief is outside the boundaries of the law, that would make you my commander in chief. I'm not going anywhere but where you order me to go, Sir."

Rockwell, "I was hoping you'd say that Jim."

Just two days ago Rockwell had met with Travis Loki - the General now has a rogue mission. He must have a private meeting with General Drew Legend, DHS (Department of Homeland Security) to raise his concerns. Currently, Rockwell has no way of knowing if Drew is aware of Project Clearcut.

Staff Sargent Wright did his research and informed Rockwell that General Drew Legend had been a career marine and staunch conservative dedicated to the Corp, now in the role of Secretary of the Department of Homeland Security. Wright had reviewed numerous speeches by General Legend and press conferences delivered as Secretary of the DHS. Wright was also able to review General Legend's business itineraries which yielded nothing appearing to indicate a relationship within the DComm Group membership.

In General Rockwell's mind, if Drew was part of that group, it would seem like he would have been in the meetings when the whole virus release thing happened. But he's never seen Drew's name on any meeting list involving the bio-weapon, so it was a pretty safe bet he wasn't involved. If he was, well it would sure be the end of Rockwell's career, but it was a chance that had to be taken.

What he knew was that he had a list, from NSA.Med.VACC.gov that showed Drew Legend's name to receive the AVBW#D, which was equal to a death sentence. He also had a copy of the mission statement for Project Clearcut which stated the plan to eliminate targeted lists of the population utilizing genocide perpetrated through the use of a virus falsely represented as a bio-weapon to be used against enemy combatants and a thorough dossier of this plan to replace the Democratic Republic of the United States with a Marxist regime.

Of course, if Legend was part of it, he already knew that, but if Wright is right, Legend will be the newest recruit to the Savior Unit.

Rockwell, "General Legend, this is General Alan Rockwell. Would like to meet with you, maybe meet for a drink?"

Legend, "Well sure General – is there something going on that needs to be off the record? I'm not very far away from the Pentagon, I could be there in twenty minutes if it would be easier."

Rockwell, "Better away, Sir, lunch or dinnertime – whatever is good for you…"

Legend, "Ok how about The Skydome – 1900 hours?"

Rockwell, "Roger, General Legend, will be there, thank you, sir."

DREW LEGEND

Drew Legend (DHS D.C.) was a career Marine with more than thirty years of service in the Corps appointed four years ago as Secretary to the Department of Homeland Security.

Rockwell had his Staff Sgt. James Wright – drop him off a block from The Skydome and told him to return in one hour to pick him up at the restaurant front door. Drew Legend was waiting in the front lobby and they went in together to the secluded table reserved by Rockwell. Rockwell orders scotch for them each then begins his pitch. It's all or nothing for him at this point, he can't let the DComm Group keep killing.

Rockwell, "General Legend I'm pretty good at shooting from the hip – but I don't know quite where to start. You have seen in the media the numbers of people dying from the virus spreading across the United States right?"

Legend, "Yes, General, a deaf and blind person would know about this, plus I'm in the thick of things in DHS."

Rockwell, "Well, Sir, please call me Alan, has anyone in the government discussed the issue with you?"

Legend, "Alan. From what I'm told it is an issue for

CDC to deal with and the medical community, I've made inquiries, but the responses seem to be pretty much the same – viral epidemic is not a security issue, none the less I am actively watching things with the crime rate and protests ramping up."

Rockwell, "General, have you been vaccinated for the virus?"

Legend, "Not yet, it seems like the problem is mostly the other side of the country. Why do you ask?"

Rockwell, "I need to tell you the story that I know to be true:

There was, in Texas, a virus developed – it was contracted by the DOD and reportedly intended to be used on enemy combatants, on foreign soil. It is a vile bug – and against the rules of war. I know that you are aware of the rules of engagement prohibiting bio-weapon use. But this bug was designed to look like something natural rather than a bio-weapon. The Army was supposed to begin field testing behind enemy lines. But…"

Legend, "Oh, I don't like the sound of this. Did this bug get loose in the USA? I've seen media coverage of the epidemic, but the media seems to suggest it was an extremely bad new strain of the flu virus. No hint that it was anything unnatural like a weapon."

Rockwell continued his narrative, "But the army never received the virus for testing…I'm going to show you something that only a very small number of people in D.C. know about." He removed a printed copy of the Project Clearcut Mission statement from his jacket pocket and handed it to Drew. "This is the true reason for the bio-weapon, Sir, it is intended to kill from 30-50% of the population of the United States.

Whatever you do General Legend, do not get, or allow any person you care about to get the vaccine – what the medical community is unwittingly doing is vaccinating people with a deadly virus to kill, not protect them. I took a chance coming to you on this...."

Legend, "Alan – I'm sorry – I am having a hard time finding any words to respond to this news – do you have any idea who all is involved in this Clearcut plan?"

Rockwell, "What I know for sure is that Chuck Delphi (DOD), Stephanie Wolff (NSA), Michael Carver (FBI), Darla Avery (CIA), and Former Director Roger Ackinsen have been deeply involved in the project. We have it on good authority that Ackinsen was killed by an order from Darla Avery."

Legend, "The car explosion thing was ordered by CIA? How high does this go?"

Rockwell, "Sir, to the top. We believe, however, that VP Hominy is unaware."

Legend, "Who are we?"

Rockwell, "We are Savior Unit, Sir, a small group of people who know the truth and are trying to put a stop to the genocide. The reason I took the risk to contact you was because of your absence from any meetings involving discussion of the bio-weapon. This made me think – no pray – that you were not involved. We need to find out who, in D.C., is in the Project Clearcut power circle, to which we refer as the DComm Group. And we need to protect those who are not. We have some plans in place regarding the virus, but if we don't find a way to cut off the heads of the DComm Group, it won't do us any good."

Legend, "Well I am NOT in that group and I will start a private search to see who else is not involved. As to the Vice President, I have to ask why you think he would be outside the circle?"

Rockwell explained the varieties of vaccines being distributed including the meanings of the #S, #G, and #D.

Rockwell, "We also know that POTUS vaccine is designated #D to be decommissioned, the VP's vaccine – already received was #G, in other words, he was designated to be saved. We believe they intend to assassinate POTUS and then just pull the strings of Hominy until they elect one of the DComm Group in the next election."

Legend, "Why would they assassinate POTUS if she is part of the circle?"

Rockwell, "We don't know yet, Sir. She is POTUS, but she's only one of the heads, she is not the controlling body. We can only speculate why they would want to be rid of her, perhaps she has served her purpose – or wants more power than the group is willing to give her. We don't have all the answers to the power structure within the group."

Rockwell hands a copy of a single page of names and vaccine designations. Drew Legend's name is highlighted along with the highlighted vaccine designated for him - it has the AVBW #D next to the vaccine.

Legend, "Does this list indicate that I am targeted for 'decommissioning' by virus?"

Rockwell, "Yes General Legend, Sir, we would suggest that you do not schedule your vaccination. I would caution you to be extremely careful who you speak with." He handed a blank white card with a handwritten phone number. "Here's my card with my number. Please do not call me on anything but a secure phone. It might serve you best to get a 'use and toss' phone to avoid being tracked. Remember that the director of the NSA is one of the heads of the DComm Group. But please contact me if you find others in, or outside, the circle that you are certain about their allegiance."

Legend, "Well where do I sign up to get the real anti-virus vaccination for myself and my family?"

Rockwell, "This virus is not like a flu virus, it doesn't get communicated by cough or sneezing, it is injected on purpose. Please make sure your family doesn't get vaccinated at this time. I'm in the process of gaining access to large quantities of what we know to be true anti-virus serum, but right now, your safest bet is to not receive any injection."

Rockwell looking at his watch, "My driver should be waiting. Do you need a ride someplace?" He put some cash on the table for their drinks.

Legend, "No thank you, Alan, I have a car waiting for me. I will be calling you soon. You can be sure that you have my support and I will be starting some of my research to find out who's on first..."

Rockwell, "If you need supporting evidence, contact me before anyone else. I have access to the designation of vaccine codes to provide you with supporting evidence of their intent, such as I provided to you about your designation. My name is on that same list, with a #D next to it also, but I understand the reason for their desire to be rid of me. I won't agree to be involved in the enactment of martial law, which is their plan."

Legend, "Could you speculate why I would be targeted for death?"

Rockwell, "Their goal is to obtain power and destroy democracy at any price. Would you be a willing party to genocide? If not, then I guess that would be your answer."

The two men exchange a firm handshake and part ways.

It didn't take long for General Legend to make arrangements to engage in communications with Rankin, Josh, and Joanna as he began working his clandestine DC advocacy with the Savior Unit.

JILL RIDER – (HHS)

Doctor Jill Rider has only recently returned to work. She had been on FMLA since the death of her 12-year-old daughter, Amee. When you have an 'at-risk child' such as her daughter, afflicted with Downs Syndrome, you make sure to protect with all vaccinations and proactive doctor's visits. Being at the head of Health and Human Services (HHS), she had seen the epidemic and immediately received her AVBW#G vaccination as well as scheduled the first available appointment with Amee's pediatrician. Two days after Amee's HVD vaccination, she had died from encephalitis. The best specialists in D.C. could do nothing to save her.

General Drew Legend was aware of the Rider family loss and had the target list of D.C. officials and their families. It was clear that the child had been targeted leaving the parents protected. He had even attended the private funeral weeks before he came to the knowledge of HVD and Project Clearcut.

He scheduled a meeting with Jill armed with the materials he'd received when he'd been recruited to the Savior Unit. The Project Clearcut Mission statement and a copy of the portion of the NSAMedVacc list showing Jill and her husband's vaccine designated as #G and Amee's being ordered as #D.

Legend, "Dr. Rider, let me say again that I'm sorry for your loss of Amee. No parent should have to bury a child. I was at the funeral but didn't want to intrude. I was surprised to hear that you had returned to work under the circumstances."

Jill, "Thank you General, I was aware of your presence and appreciate your kind discretion. As to my return to work, I guess hard work can be therapeutic in dealing with pain. There is so much going on with the epidemic, it just made sense for me to spend my days doing something good for someone else rather than dwell on the things I can't change. What is it I may assist the Department of Homeland Security with?

Legend, "Doctor, the only way I can explain my desire for this meeting, is to provide you with some information, then try to answer your questions."

He then put in front of Dr. Jill Rider a stapled packet of information similar to the one he'd received when he was recruited by General Rockwell. Jill quickly reviewed the packet's contents, her mouth slightly open as she absorbed the shocking material in front of her.

Jill, "General. Legend, does Rankin CDC have this information? This shows that my daughter was targeted for death by virus."

Legend, "I'm sorry Dr. Rider, but you have before you the proof of this fact. It was Rankin that wanted me to enlist your assistance, he's best described as 'stuck' between the axis of good and evil in this matter. As long as they don't know he is working to expose the truth, he is safe from removal or worse."

Jill, "Well how the hell can we make it stop? This is insane, the stuff you see in banana republics, not the United States of America!"

Legend, "We have people who are getting the distribution centers under control but there are quantities of the #D serum, the lethal virus, already in possession of the medical centers and clinics across the country. The Savior Unit is a small group and we don't have the assets to reach such a large population of providers."

Jill, "Well, General Legend, I DO have access! I will prepare a nationwide directive to recall all existing #D vaccine and to cease all vaccinations until the suspect #D is completely recalled. Where in the government am I going to get pushback?"

Legend, "The President, Dr. Rider. It will probably cost your job."

Jill "I've lost the most precious part of my life, my daughter. Do you think I give a shit about my job working for a government that would target 'at risk' children?"

Legend, "Dr. Rider it isn't the entire government, only a handful of very sick people. What Savior is planning is to first get the virus contained, and then go after the DComm Group to prevent them from causing further damage."

Jill, "How long do you think I'll have before the President discovers my directive to the medical community?"

Legend, "We have some assets inside NSA who can at least delay the discovery if they know when you issue the directive."

Jill, "I'll need two days to collect the medical facility lists...."

Legend, "I can get you a complete list in 10 minutes from our NSA assets, we have tools..."

Jill, "Great, then I will prepare the directive today and launch it tomorrow morning if I have received the list. Will your assets be able to keep a lid on it for forty-eight hours?"

Legend, "Consider it done, Dr. Rider. And I am extremely sorry for your loss. I've written my phone number on the back of my card please contact me on this number only from a secure phone. We have NSA monitoring agents involved so if your name comes up in the system, it will be snatched and records destroyed. We use disposable phones to avoid detection."

Jill, "Thank you, General Legend. I will pick up several phones on my way back to the office. You have my support and allegiance to stop this insanity. This is the one thing I can do to vindicate my angel."

Drew Legend departs and immediately advises Dave Tillis to provide Dr. Jill Rider anything she needs to issue the directive and to ensure that her issue is kept away from all but trusted Savior assets for as long as possible.

JOSH AND BETH

All government employees must receive the vaccine but...

Josh and Beth have been busy – not just compiling numbers of deaths, but comparing the deaths with the #character of virus the deceased received. They have charts and graphs which got them nowhere. But when they charted the deaths related to the type of vaccine the deceased had received, there was suddenly a surge of knowledge. The fact that deaths occurred in patients who received the AVBW#D had been established weeks ago, but they discovered new information linking the targeting lists to the NSA. It was the NSA who was distributing the lists to medical providers.

The next step was to identify the relational data between #D and #S medical delivery. The #D deaths primarily were ill, long-time unemployed, entitlement recipients, or disabled. In the category of previously employed HVD deaths, there was a significantly higher number in the field of law enforcement. They decided it was best to include the #G serum distribution list and found that the entire list included people who were employed in government jobs.

To summarize:

AVBW#D targets people who are as stated in the Project Clearcut Mission statement, non-contributional people.

AVBW#S Saves lives temporarily as it is a placebo.

AVBW#G is mandatory to save governmental employees.

But Josh thinks, *Not all government employees are targeted to receive the #G serum. I have to find out the difference between government employees who received or are targeted with the #D serum.* Whatever possessed him to bring this up to Beth? He didn't know, but he did it anyway.

Josh, "Beth we need to put our heads together on this... it's sort of a riddle ok? Hypothetical ok? If we have five hundred government employees all five hundred are required to receive vaccines, three hundred live, two hundred of them die. They are all employed and healthy - tell me why did two hundred die viral death?"

Beth, "Are they redheads?"

Josh, "Very funny Beth – I've eliminated financial status, health status, entitlement status, age, and hair color....."

Beth, "Well did they pay their taxes?"

Josh, "Come on Beth this is a real puzzle that needs to be solved. My brain is swimming."

Beth, "Well my aunt used to say the only thing a person can't avoid is death and taxes even though that's not good politics to say............"

Josh, "WHAT did you just say?"

Beth, "Death and taxes ....did they pay their taxes? Do you need a nap?"

Josh, "No you said politics – holy shit I need to find out if the NSA.med.vac website has voter registration records in the criteria list – BETH I think you might be a little bit genius..............."

"Nope', said Beth, 'it's just the luck of the Irish!" Her red swirls of curls danced to the beat, in her head, as she danced a few steps of an Irish jig.

He was shaking his head in wonderment – she had a way of pulling a rabbit out of the hat with the simplest observations. And sure as God made little green apples, when he revised his search of government employees, he discovered not all government employees received the #G. When he re-sorted the government list by political voter affiliation – he found that the ones who were scheduled to receive the #D serum were ALL registered republicans.

NSA/MED/VACC.GOV

Stephanie Wolff visits monitoring to bring a request to Beau Clark. "Beau, I need to add another name to search and listen for Barbara Kaye Foster M.E. in addition to previous MSA121068, Joshua Klein, and Beth McCallum. That's Miss Barbara Kaye Foster from Dallas/ Fort Worth TX area."

Beau, "Yes Maam, added to the list. I will CC Dave Tillis in medical monitoring if you want me to ma'am, he is watching for McCallum and Klein to see if they get vaccinated or dead."

Stephanie, "Good man – thank you. It will be nice when we can get these crazies rounded up and get back to normal."

Beau, "Yes Maam, you sure –'nuff are sayin' the truth about that crazy stuff goin' on round us, ma'am."

Stephanie, "I'm thinking I will owe you dinner or something special when we get this crazy stuff over with…."

Beau, "Yes Ma'am, Nuthin' finer than spendin' some quality time with the finest lady in the country. I'd be honored to go to dinner with you Miss Wolff."

Stephanie, "I'm thinking since you are from Louisiana, perhaps you would enjoy some Cajun food."

Beau, "Yes ma'am, I sure do love Cajun, but I don't think I've ever found any here in Utah ma'am."

Stephanie, "Well then, perhaps we will just have to take the jet to Louisiana one of these weekends soon."

Beau, "Well hush muh puppies' ma'am, that's a mighty generous offer!"

Stephanie liked the Ragin Cajun. He was young and certainly on the fringe of anything that seemed normal to her, but that kinky uniqueness made her want to do things.... She knew she was beautiful and desired by every man who ever laid eyes on her. Those men weren't the slightest bit interesting to her. But she'd take on a whole Ragin Cajun army if they were all fringe like this Beau Clark. She made herself blush when she thought like that. Yes – she had to admit to herself – she had a weakness for the fringe. This boy toy wouldn't be good for much anything after she was finished with him. She'd better get out of this room right now, she was fantasizing too much for her own good. Yes, she would take him to the place of voodoo and primal behavior. *Soon* she thinks.....

The death toll list from Dave Tillis goes to Stephanie Wolff weekly. She has however directed him to red flag Joshua Klein and Beth McCallum to make sure she is advised immediately if either of them shows up at any medical facility or turns up dead.

"Yes, Miss Wolff," *no questions asked as I stay under the radar,* thinks Dave.

Tillis will change the entry in the database to show that Josh and Beth received their #D vaccines in Cleveland Clinic, no death was recorded. He then covers his tracks by executing a database translation log file which removes his access and changes to the database program. In another life, Dave Tillis was a 'black hat' hacker, so he knows well how to cover his tracks. The next order of business is to send the report to Miss Wolff after-hours, 1900 hours Eastern Standard Time precisely.

Seconds after receiving the report, Stephanie forwards the message to Carver (FBI). The message he won't be receiving until 0900 EST tomorrow morning. Of course, Carver's next step is to call the Cleveland FBI offices.

Cleveland Clinic database shows immunizations #D given to Joshua Klein and Beth McCallum with records showing scans of their driver's licenses, but no other information. The FBI agents must now begin searching all of Cleveland and outlying medical facilities to try to locate them or death reports on the two.

When Joshua saw the NSA report of the Cleveland immunizations, he smiled and thought, *Well played David – well played!*

Goose however was confused (if a droid could be confused). Joshua and Beth were here not in Cleveland, were they going to be decommissioned?

Goose, "Josh in Cleveland - Beth in Cleveland - decommissioned? Must save humanity - must save Josh - must save Beth. Explain please."

Josh puts his hand on Goose's arm and says, "It's ok Goose, the report is false."

Goose, "Oh subterfuge?

> Webster, deception, fraud, double-dealing, and trickery.

Goose, "Is this correct?"
Josh, "Yes Goose, that is correct – Webster?"
Goose, "Goose has tools."

Dave Tillis is monitoring viral deaths in states that are spreading out around the distribution hub locations. His data is feeding directly to Goose which is uploading to Josh for charts, graphs, and strategy planning.

Beau is monitoring any activity related to the search

patterns for Beth and Josh and now Barbara Foster M.E. He is also doctoring the death count reports intended for the director. Miss Wolff wants daily reports of viral deaths. This information is being collected by his buddy Dave Tillis and it is part of Beau's job to doctor the reports for Miss Wolff's eyes. The numbers are going down but Beau's reports do not reflect the decline.

Joanna said, seeing the slowdown of the deaths will put their mission at risk. It would make the DComm Group suspicious of their plan being infiltrated. The Savior Unit could not risk suspicion. They needed to save lives and find the sympathizers to stop the genocide being perpetrated against the U.S. population.

IN PLAIN SIGHT MILWAUKEE, WI

Allen Smitt reporting Milwaukee Wisconsin, WITI, Antenna TV.

"I'm Allen Smitt – reporting the news – In Plain Sight. Today I need to talk about this virus – the epidemic that is racing across our nation and the insane reaction to it."

Allen has a split-screen – the other screen shows the riots in the streets of large cities across the USA – bold name banners beneath each new video clip that rolls on.

"People are dying – here – in the largest cities of the United States people are dying from the freezing temperatures in the upper Midwest and Northeast. And they are dying in California, Texas, Florida, and warm climate locations from heat strokes. And where the exposure to the extreme elements isn't killing them, they are dying from violence perpetrated by their fellow citizens who are there in the lines, for the same reason, to try to save their lives from a virus whose origin even the CDC refuses to identify.

What we are not hearing is anyone talking about the question of how people are dying when they have received these precious antivirus vaccinations that they are willing to fight in the streets for.

I have personal knowledge of family and friends who have died after receiving the anti-virus. So what we are investigating at WITI, is the number of deaths of those people who have received the anti-virus. The mainstream media posts streaming Public Service. Announcements encouraging people to get these vaccinations – but nobody is showing any statistics to indicate the effectiveness of the vaccines."

Allen continues, "I have with me today, Dr. Trish Mason. Thank you for joining us In Plain Sight today."

Dr. Mason, "Thank you for having me on, Allen."

Allen, "So Doctor Mason, what can you tell us about the virus and the vaccination process?"

Dr. Mason, "Well Allen, the virus is still a mystery to the medical community – it starts with what appears to be a common cold, and subsequently seems to go wild attacking different essential systems in the body, aggressively breaking down internal organs until the host, um, the patient dies."

Allen, "And the vaccination process? Is this a drug that is supposed to kill the virus or prevent the virus from attacking?"

Dr. Mason, "The anti-virus is intended to prevent the virus from incubating in the human host that has been exposed."

Allen, "You say 'intended'- are you saying that the anti-virus isn't working as it is supposed to? Or are there some people who are resistant to the anti-virus?"

Dr. Mason, "Well Allen, this is where the medical community is struggling for answers. They aren't privy to computational data that would be able to determine the answer to your questions as to whether the anti-virus is not working or something else. What we need is a comprehensive study to try to identify the relational data between those who died from the virus with and without the administration of the vaccine. What I have started is a national website that is requesting family and friends of those who have died in suspected or diagnosed viral infection, to fill out a simple form that will help us collect enough data to develop a model. There is a section that includes questions of those who have received the anti-virus and have been protected also. This will help us identify a possible problem with any of the anti-virus vaccines – there are multiple formulae you know…."

Allen, "No I was not aware that there were multiple formulae. Doctor, you are aware that the mainstream media considers any suggestion of challenging the effectiveness of the anti-virus as conspiracy theory right?"

Dr. Mason, "Yes Allen, I am aware of this, but the evidence we have collected in our local target area suggests that there may be supportive proof of a possible conspiracy. This data will help to prove or disprove the conspiracy. Of course, we hope the conspiracy theory is wrong. We are approaching this from a purely empirical perspective. Our ultimate goal is to determine the demonstrative effectiveness of the vaccine."

Allen, "Well Dr. Mason, if a conspiracy is proven as a result of your study, we have much more to fear than an epidemic. Will you tell us the name of your very important website?"

Dr. Mason, "Of course Allen, it is wwwDrMasonVirusStudy.net ."

Allen, "We will have your website posted on our WITI TV homepage and our Facebook page as well. I hope you get great information to solve this burning question and please rejoin us with your compiled results. I look forward to your follow up visit. Thank you so much for joining us Doctor Mason and for bringing this very important information to 'In Plain Sight' today. I'm Allen Smitt, and I'd like to thank my viewing audience for being here – where our goal is as always to view the truth 'In Plain Sight'."

* * *

www.DrMasonVirusStudy.net

"Thank you for visiting our website, this endeavor intends to collect information regarding the administration of the AVBW anti-virus vaccine. Your information will be kept confidential. The data you provide will not be shared with any agency or organization.

We have strived to make this questionnaire as simple to use as possible. Just click the appropriate answer and fill in the remaining fields. A comment section is available for you to share any additional information or observations you may have regarding your experience."

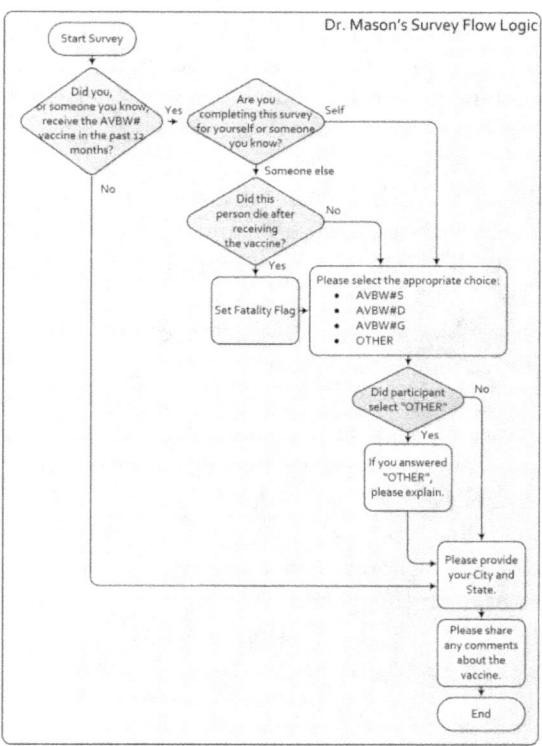

"Thank you for answering these vaccination questions. To assist us with collecting the maximum amount of data, please share the link with others you know, who have been vaccinated within the last 12 months. The data collected could help save lives.

All responses are confidential."

* * *

Savior Unit

This WITI television interview is exactly the type of reporting that Beth has been watching for.

Josh, "We need to find a way for him to help Dr. Trish Mason disseminate and promote the web link to other major cities to get more data."

Beth, "I can create false Facebook, Twitter, and Instagram accounts and begin sharing the www.DrMasonVirusStudy.net link – and perhaps start a blog – BUGGER BLOG."

Josh, "Facebook, Google, Instagram, and Twitter will probably catch those and shut them down, but once started –the retweets, chats and such could be too much to be controlled by those platforms. We don't want to waste our time and energy on stuff that will get beaten down before we get any real traction."

Beth, "Oh this one is a good one – I love it. How about a phony law firm – 'if YOU (this made her giggle hysterically – like a dead person could make the call) or someone you know died after receiving the AVBW vaccination call 1800BADVIRUS or go to the website www.badvirus.com link shown at the bottom of the screen.

We would need to pay for the television ad, but you know that anytime someone sees that ad, they will go there to see if they might be 'entitled to receive a substantial settlement'."

Josh, "Beth – how do you do that? You just pulled

another rabbit out of the hat."

Beth does her little Irish Jig dance steps and giggles her silly little laugh.

Josh sends the video ad 800BADVIRUS concept to Joanna to see if there is a way to fund it and keep the purchase anonymous.

Joanna, "That sounds like a job for Art. Funding is no problem, but it will need to come from a false legal firm."

Josh, "The website reference will roll the respondent directly to the www.DrMasonVirusStudy.net which we are already monitoring. The 800 number can go directly to an answering system telling the caller that the first step in qualifying to make a claim is to go to the Dr. Mason virus study.net site. I don't think we need a call center, we just need an automated message that directs the caller to the website so we can get people to respond to that questionnaire. We can set up the rollover links."

Joanna, "Great ideas there, Josh, will you contact Art and get the ball rolling, he can message me when he gets a funding requirements list. The ad can be a simple text screen with a voice-over message? Do you and Beth want to make the TV ad?"

Josh, "Sure thing, Joanna."

CAPUBLICAN

"Good afternoon and thank you for listening to CApublican – the California radio station where the 'the conservative viewpoint is alive and well'. My name is Hooper Dawson and for the next hour, we need to be discussing the truth about the HVD virus that is sweeping the country.

Our talking point today is what the liberal media has been calling a viral conspiracy. There is nothing further from the truth when it comes to the discussion of the virus and more importantly the vaccination process. There is no conspiracy theory coming from CApublican radio."

Hooper continues, "I have on the phone, Dr. Trish Mason. Thank you for joining us, Doctor. We understand that you have been evaluating data you have received regarding the correlation between the sweeping numbers of deaths as it is related to the number and types of vaccines being distributed across the country. Can you please enlighten us on what you are seeing?"

Dr. Mason, "Thank you, Hooper, I would first say to your listening audience, that it is important to keep this data collection coming as long as the viral deaths continue. But to date, what we are seeing is absolute empirical data indicating that the viral deaths have a definite link to the receipt of vaccination of the 'anti-virus' vaccinations. When I speak publicly on this topic, I use air quotes around the word 'anti-virus' and I will tell you the reason. The statistics based on the public response to the website questionnaire at www.DrMasonvirusstudy.net, indicate that the suggestion by the liberal media that this virus to vaccine relationship is merely a conspiracy theory is wrong."

Hooper, "If I understand what you are suggesting here, is that the anti-virus vaccinations are causing the deaths."

Dr. Mason, "Yes, Hooper, that is exactly what the statistics have shown."

Hooper, "So are you saying it is in the best interest of the country to stop getting the vaccinations?"

Dr. Mason, "Yes, Hooper."

Hooper, "Wow, that's asking a lot of our listeners. To suggest that they do not get their vaccinations!"

Dr. Mason, "Hooper, I realize this sounds extreme, but I have the data based on responses number in the hundreds of thousands."

Hooper: "Let's take some callers, our lines are all lit up. Caller, what is your first name, and what is your question for Dr. Trish Mason?"

Caller, "Hi, my name is Sherrie, my question for Dr. Mason is this: I have children who have received the vaccination for the HVD virus and had no problems even though we know people who have had family who has died from the virus – this would seem that the anti-virus is working. So how do you respond to this information?"

Dr. Mason, "Thank you, Sherrie, this is a good question. There are multiple vaccine serums. If you go to the website, you would see that. I suspect that your provider could tell you the specific #ID of the vaccine your children received. What our empirical evidence is showing that the vaccine identified as AVBW#S is one of the three and seems to be unrelated to viral deaths."

Caller Sherrie, "Well my provider told me that based on their database we were all supposed to receive the #S vaccine!"

Dr. Mason, "Sherrie, that means that your family was designated to be protected, at this time, from the virus."

Hooper, "Thank you Sherrie for your call. Next caller please…"

Caller Jackson, "My name is Jackson. I have a brother who was in law enforcement. He received the #D vaccine and died within twelve days after receiving it. I have an uncle who works for the sewer district and his vaccine was #G and he's doing just fine. Can you explain why family members would receive different types of vaccines? I'm sort of hesitating about getting any vaccine at all."

Dr. Mason, "Jackson, not getting any vaccine at this point is probably the wisest decision. We are still collecting information, but we currently have sufficient data to state with clarity that the #D is absolutely a death-causing vaccine. The #G seems to be a true anti-virus to protect selected government workers."

Caller Jackson, "Doctor, why would the government want to kill a member of law enforcement? Our streets are swarming with criminals committing crimes with impunity because of a reduced presence of police!"

Dr. Mason, "Was your brother a republican?"

Jackson is now disconnected.

Hooper, "We seemed to have lost Jackson. Doctor Mason, the information you have brought us today is pretty overwhelming. Could I ask you to stay with us for a while longer? During our commercial break, I'm going to see if my producer will let us go on to an extended segment. Our incoming caller board is going into meltdown."

After the break, Hooper continues, "We're back, Thanks to our listening audience for staying with us. We are talking with Doctor Trish Mason about her recent data collection related to the deaths associated with the vaccinations against what some people are now referring to as the HVD virus. Doctor Mason, to refresh what we were talking about in our last segment please correct me if my summary is unclear:

There are three different vaccines: AVBW#S which seems to be a life-saving anti-virus, AVBW#G which appears to be an anti-virus that does offer protection for people working for the government, and AVBW#D which your data shows is a virus – NOT an anti-virus but a lethal killing virus. This is very unsettling news Doctor – if I have understood what you are reporting."

Dr. Mason, "What you said is correct except for the #S – the #S seems to do nothing at all."

Hooper, "I'm sorry?"– I thought the #S saved people as the ones who got it didn't die from it…"

Dr. Mason, "Hooper, the #S doesn't appear to be a vaccine; what we are seeing is the possibility of it being a temporary 'stay' of execution of sorts."

Hooper, "Doctor Mason – you said STAY OF EXECUTION? We need to take a short commercial break here and when we return we will be clarifying this stay and we will be taking more questions from our CApublican audience."

But the CApublican program did not return from the commercial break. Their building was stormed by a military contingent. They would no longer be broadcasting 'Conservative viewpoint – alive and well'.

Hooper Dawson in California had managed to call Dr. Mason from his cell phone before he was taken someplace unknown. She quickly called the data office manager to warn them to get all evidence of the www.DrMasonVirusStudy.net out of the building and find a way to get it securely to Dr. Rankin of the CDC. She didn't care if they had to drive the information to Texas, it needed to get out of Minnesota before the military had time to break into their offices.

The CApublican program was being monitored by the Savior Unit......

* * *

Savior Unit

Josh, "HOLY CRAP! BETH! You are not going to believe this!"

Beth, "What's happened? Are you ok?"

Josh, "Remember when I told you about that cable tv show called 'In Plain Sight' the one that had Dr. Mason who put up the website to collect data? You worked on charting some of the data right?"

Beth, "Yes, it was good information, what happened?"

Josh, "Well I had contacted her and begged her to get more visibility, right? She was just on a radio broadcast, some conservative broadcast from California – called CApublican.

She was talking about the results of the virus study and saying what we already know that the HVD is killing not protecting. But right in the middle of the show – the radio station got stormed by a group of military people and the show host was taken out at gunpoint!"

Beth, "OMG! Is there any further news about the broadcaster?"

Josh, "Nothing yet – I'm going to text Dave Tillis and see if he's gotten anything on this."

Beth, "Is Goose with you – monitoring?"

Josh, "Yes, wait, Goose, have you gotten any media information about Dr. Mason?"

Goose, "`Yes Joshua Goose, Dr. Mason on WITI with Allen Smitt. Doctor has fear.`"

Josh, "Thank you Goose. Did you hear that Beth? I've gotta go follow up on WITI. We might need to bring Dr. Mason in."

Beth, "How can I help?"

Josh, "Sit tight, you might be getting a roomie."

Josh, "Goose, can you please find me a private cell number for Dr. Trish Mason?"

Goose, "Yes   Joshua   friend¬   Must   save humanity.   Must save Dr. Mason?"

Josh, "Yes, Goose."

IN PLAIN SIGHT - FOLLOWUP

Allen Smitt reporting Milwaukee Wisconsin – WITI – Antenna TV

"I'm Allen Smitt – reporting – In Plain Sight. In breaking news today, we have Doctor Trish Mason with us. Her fascinating story from last week has taken a new twist that we at WITI Milwaukie felt was imperative to bring to our viewing audience."

Allen has a split-screen – the other screen shows men dressed in all black riot gear, lacking any agency identifiers, bearing assault weapons surrounding a small building in California. The building bears the name CAPublican Radio Studios. Several people are being marched out the front door with their hands raised above their heads – the sidewalk to the parking area is lined with armed men. As the camera pans the front of the building, there are other black-clad men with weapons trained on the employees with their raised hands.

"This is the scene just minutes ago at the radio station home to CAPublican – a conservative radio station. What I'm getting in my ear is information telling me that during their broadcast with Doctor Trish Mason, an armed paramilitary group stormed the offices, interrupting the radio program IN PROGRESS, as they were discussing Doctor Mason's proof that the virus killing U.S. citizens is not an accident, but a deliberate plan for the government to commit genocide on the population!"

"Fortunately, Doctor Mason was conferenced in for this radio broadcast and she was not arrested with the show host, Hooper Dawson."

"I now have a video conference with Dr. Mason. Doctor, I hope you are in a very secure location. Thank you so much for calling this information to us at In Plain Sight News. Rather than my asking you questions, I will just ask you to tell us what you know, because I realize your safety could be in jeopardy with this knowledge and time is of the essence."

Dr. Mason, "Thank you, Allen, I was sharing this information over the radio broadcast with CAPublican when that group breached their office, and the broadcast was shut down. I don't know if the broadcast was captured for purposes of replay that is why I felt I needed to contact you. If your station can capture the content of the radio broadcast, it would be a good thing.

I will try to be as brief as possible to convey my message to the American people. The study we did on the vaccination brought empirical data to indicate that the vaccines reported by the government as a treatment against a deadly virus, are vaccines that target select groups of citizens for death based on financial, health, or political affiliation. The safest thing for people to do is to not receive any vaccine for any reason."

Allen, "I'm sorry to interrupt Doctor – did you say POLITICAL affiliation was a factor?"

Dr. Mason, "Yes, Allen – political, in addition to people who are recipients of entitlement programs for example disability and welfare recipients. We discovered that welfare, food stamps, and controlled income housing recipients are required to get vaccinated for the continued qualification of existing or to receive new benefits. What I'm saying Allen, is that the government is in the process of committing an act of genocide on citizens that have been determined to be a burden to the economy. Excuse me, Allen, I'm getting a message….."

Dr. Mason continued, "Oh I'm so sorry, it seems that my offices are being raided by a similarly clad group at this minute."

Allen, "OH MY GOD, Doctor, are you alright? Is your proof going to be seized?"

Dr. Mason, "I'm ok right now Allen, and we have the data, but I think I should leave now."

Allen, "Well please be safe Dr. Mason, and thank you for bringing this breaking news to share with our viewing audience. WITI has on our website a link to view today's show in addition to our previous show hosting Doctor Mason and the breaking news of the CAPublican breach. I encourage our viewing audience to record and share these video links with friends and family. It is important to get this information disseminated to the public. We don't know how long it will take the government to try to take our website down, so please share this information as soon as possible.

We will continue to monitor breaking news as it happens, and pray that we can be part of an effort to save the country from heading into, what appears to be, a dictatorial regime.

Thank you to my viewing audience for being here – where our goal is as always to bring the truth 'In Plain Sight'."

This program – like the CAPublican radio broadcast was viewed and recorded by the Savior Unit.

It was also picked up by the Associated Press and was now being rebroadcast on every news channel in the United

States of America. Just seconds after Dr. Mason disconnected her call to Allen Smitt, her phone rang from the anonymous caller. It was Joshua Klein calling to ask where he could collect her to take her to the safety of the Savior Unit. She is in Minnesota, so it is probably impossible for her to get a flight anywhere with the data she has removed from her offices in Minnesota.

Josh asked Dr. Mason if she can get to Minneapolis. She said yes – it is only about a 40-minute drive.

"Great' says Josh, 'I'm going to give you an address to an Army National Guard facility. Show your identification at the gate tell them that General Yabo is expecting you. You will be escorted to an office where you can share the data you have saved from your offices and you will then be escorted by military transport to Texas where we will pick you up and bring you to a secure location. Someone here will be waiting for you and make arrangements for your safety – they will get your data to us and provide you a safe shelter until we can get you moved to a safe house. Since your offices were breached, it is probably best if you don't go to your home. Once you get to Texas, we will see that you have clothing and whatever personal needs you have."

Dr. Mason, "But it was some kind of military group that breached CApublican and my offices.

Josh, "Dr. Mason, your safety is extremely important to us. You will be meeting General Yabo, and your safety will be guaranteed."

ANNIE OAKDALE

Joanna reassigned Annie Oakdale from RiverMoore to manage the lab control division over at Bearlywoke Storage.

Annie's job is monitoring to ensure that the only Bearlywoke inventory is the Cool Aid variety labeled as AVBW#Ss. Over the three months of mislabeling Cool Aid as antivirus, the actual anti-virus AV_JMV2030 has been moved to a very secret location only known to an MSA droid and its handler.

Until they are sure that there is no chance of an active virus somewhere, it is far too risky to have no anti-virus inventory stored. Unfortunately, during the auditing process, Annie discovered that there are some major discrepancies between the manufacturing output and the distributions to the U.S. hub warehouses. She will need to bring this to the attention of Joshua and MSA121068. The inventory discrepancy was found to be delivered to a New Mexico storage location which is currently empty.

DR. YĪSHĒNG SǏWÁNG

(FORMER DIRECTOR BEARLYWOKE)

Michael Carver (Director FBI)- on the phone with Chuck Delphi.

"Chuck, what's happening with tracking Dr. Yīshēng down?"

Delphi, "Damn if I know Mr. Carver. He just disappeared. I've had people checking everyplace, we know he took his private jet and left for Beijing, China. He left no message – no manifesto. But I found a paper trail indicating that he was sending truckloads of RMV2030, JMV2030_R, and AV_JMV2030 to a warehouse on the outskirts of Albuquerque, New Mexico."

Carver, "Oh shit – have you secured the warehouse?"

Delphi, "It's empty."

Carver, "What? You had it removed back to Bearlywoke?"

Delphi, "No, sir, it's empty. We've hit a dead-end - no paper trail where it went – my guess is that it went to Beijing, China."

Carver, "Who else knows?"

Delphi, "Nobody yet – should I call Darla?"

Carver, "Well I'm pretty sure she needs to know before Secretary of State Robert Hoge."

Delphi called Darla Avery with the news about the missing Dr. Yīshēng and serum. He was so concerned that he failed to notice how unconcerned she seemed to be.

That was because, unbeknownst to both Carver and Delphi, Darla Avery knows exactly where Yīshēng is and what his task is concerning the missing HVD virus.

* * *

Utah

Beau was taking his time preparing to inform Stephanie Wolff regarding the AP stories about Dr. Trish Mason. He knows she is going to be frosty when she hears this news so he calls Dave Tillis.

Beau, "Dude – have you seen the AP stuff about that Dr. Mason study?"

Dave, "The AP picked up her website? Shit – that's great for the people, but could be bad for her. Did you call Stephanie yet?"

Beau, "Wellllll, I was kinda hopin' you might want that honor. She's been sort of flirty with me and I don't wanna be the one to cool her jets…"

Dave, "OK but you owe me."

Dave sends an email to Stephanie, with the unhappy news. She followed up with a message to Dave to query the vaccine designation for Dr. Trish Mason and whether she'd been vaccinated yet. If not – change the records to #D order.

She thanked him and immediately forwarded the information to Delphi with her addition to the text – DR. MASON #D VACCINE or most convenient dispatch SEE TO THIS.

Chuck Delphi is not a happy camper – this isn't

something he can handle with a phone call – it is time for the situation room with Madam President and Carver. And Miss Wolff is just going to have to wait.

POTUS, DELPHI, CARVER
MARTIAL LAW

Situation room – the Whitehouse

Delphi, "Madam President, have you seen breaking news on every television station in the United States?"

POTUS, "I have people who are paid to watch television; there's so much out now Helen Keller would have been able to know what was on every television station. What the hell are we going to do about it?"

Delphi, "Well Madam President – I'm afraid you have no option at this point but to call for martial law. You can bet your lace panties that the people are going to react. You know I tried to get you to order martial law weeks ago."

POTUS, "Did you bring your letter of resignation along with your 'I told you so'? I'd be delighted to fire your ass, Director Delphi."

Carver, "Let's not be reactive here, we have options."

POTUS, "Such as?"

Carver, "Well I believe, first off, you need to sign an executive order for martial law – with no end date –

generic, to run as long as needed to resolve the unrest associated with the HVD, but PLEASE, let's make sure the term HVD is not mentioned in anything from D.C. The media is now referring to HVD as what it is, Human Decommission Virus. We cannot under any circumstances admit the true nature of the virus.

The second action I would recommend is to order the confiscation of all guns. Maybe this can be incorporated into the martial law executive order.

Both actions can be represented as a means to protect the people. They don't need to know that your gun removal means to prevent insurrection."

POTUS, "Ok that makes sense. What about body recycling programs? Have they been discovered?"

Delphi, "No they have not been discovered – yet, Madam, but I strongly suggest there is a critical need for a cover-up of that activity."

POTUS, "Who can manage that action?"

Delphi, "I'm thinking General Rockwell can handle that."

Carver, "Rockwell? Have you forgotten our discussions with him regarding martial law?"

POTUS, "Am I missing something?"

Carver, "Oh there was a discussion about the possible need for martial law. He got a little bit heated up over it."

Delphi, "He's a dick, we probably need a different general for this."

Carver, "I will talk with him, Delphi – you have a way of pushing people's buttons."

POTUS, "Okay, I will get legal on the Executive Order and my speechwriters to preparing my written and television script about the martial law and need for gun 'buyback'. It can't be a confiscation – you know some will not give up their guns. Hopefully, some of them will be willing to 'sell them'."

Delphi, "Oh Madam President, one other small action

item, Emmett Rankin – CDC is no longer needed. Any future needs of the CDC can be handled by someone else. He's much too close to HVD at this point, and it is probably best to just dump him and blame the virus release on CDC as an organizational failure to protect."

POTUS, "I will have his resignation today. Thank you, do you have a suggestion for a replacement? What about Stephanie Wolff? Is she keeping things together?"

Delphi, "Not at this time for a replacement, Madam President, but I will put some people on it for you. Perhaps someone with a medical background would be better suited for the CDC."

Carver, "Madam President, to the best of my knowledge Stephanie is holding up her end. It appears, however, that Project Clearcut documents have been leaked to the public. I wouldn't accuse Wolff of wrongdoing, but if you considered it time to thin the herd somewhat, well she serves at the pleasure…"

As soon as this brief meeting is concluded, Delphi contacted Stephanie to advise her that it might be time to depart the USA.

CARVER TO GENERAL ROCKWELL

Rockwell has seen the media coverage and he has a large contingent of the army under him awaiting orders.

Staff Sgt. Wright, "Sir, Mr. Carver – FBI on line two, do you want to take the call, sir?" Do we need this to be recorded, sir?"

Rockwell, "Yes and Yes, I'll take it thanks, Sergeant. To Carver he says, "Sir, how can I help you Mr. Carver, Sir?"

Carver, "Well, General we have some pretty bad stuff going on, I'm sure you've seen the news by now."

Rockwell, "I am aware Sir, what is it you need from us?"

Carver, "POTUS is preparing for a nationwide address. She is going to be signing an executive order to impose martial law beginning tomorrow night at midnight. The following morning she's going to throw up a website offering military transport to temporary military installations to administer the vaccines.

Rockwell, "Is that all sir?"

Carver, "She is also rolling gun confiscation into the executive order. She is going to be calling it a buyback."

Rockwell, "That's not gonna sit very well with the 2nd amendment public and the NRA, Sir. Why is the FBI calling the Army, Sir?"

Carver, "Because your commander in chief has no balls, General. I need a list of hub accessible locations with enough area for the Army to set up tent cities for this vaccination process, orders for military transports, and contingents of cyber-geeks to manage the pickup schedule."

Rockwell, "Who does she think is going to start confiscating guns, Sir?"

Carver, "She didn't say, do you want it, or do you want me to call the police or Marines?"

Rockwell, "My job is not FBI advisor, Sir. Seems like the Army is going to be pretty busy, Sir. You might find that such an order might need to come from POTUS, Sir."

Carver, "OK, I'll discuss that with her, then. Oh, General – I nearly forgot, she wants to cover up the recycling process locations."

Rockwell, "Sir, the U.S. Army is not in the business of coverups. What exactly are you proposing we do? The bodies need to be disposed of. Does she have a suggestion about what she wants to be done with them? From what I hear, most of them have no known families and many are homeless with no means of identification. Let me know if she clarifies with you what she wants. Sir."

The call is disconnected then Wright enters and gives General Rockwell a thumbs up. "Transcript already sent off to Savior Sir."

Carver's request to get the military to do the temporary immunization locations is a great opportunity to establish recruiting and educational centers. Incoming registration can sort the dissenters and recruit them for the revolution.

The others can receive their Cool Aid shots and be returned to their cities none the wiser.

But this new stuff, he has no idea what his action will be when it comes to the bodies. The ones going to medical schools for research – he could understand that. Fertilizer and animal food, hmmm that was pretty barbaric in his opinion. He's only heard rumors about the 3rd option, the recycling bodies to make food for the homeless shelters and soup kitchens. That was certainly the least civilized behavior ever perpetrated on American soil.

Rockwell, "Ok Sergeant, it's showtime, do we have people with video of the recycling centers?"

Wright, "Sir, we do have video – the fertilizer making plants, the frozen bodies in warehouses in New England for the medical school studies, and the burger factories for the homeless shelters. We've got it all on video – with great narrative - documentary style stuff – already sent to Savior and if you authorize it, Sir. I can see that this stuff goes to the temporary immunization locations also, sir. Like, recruitment centers. Will we be inoculating with real anti-virus (AVBW#G) at these locations? If so, I can get someone on picking up the serum a.s.a.p. for transfer, Sir.

It is my understanding that the burger factories are managed by droids, to minimize the number of eyes on the activity going on in those centers. I'm told that the burger is packaged to export to China, kinda hard to imagine our country doing this shit, sir."

Rockwell, "Let me get back to you on that. I think that ultimately, we will need to get all military and law enforcement vaccinated. At this point, I don't feel mass inoculations are necessary. Probably best to save any excess for possible foreign action. But put in a call to Annie Oakdale down at Bearlywoke – tell her that every Army truck that delivers HVD needs to be refilled with 50% active AVBW#G and 50% ABVW#S (Cool Aid). That way we will have serum for the troops and the civilians from each truck arriving at the temporary recruitment locations. She also needs to be advised to boost AVBW#G production. I'm going to have to think about what to do about recycling."

Wright, "Consider it done, Sir."

General Rockwell issued orders to his transport details

to begin their pickup operations. Since Bearlywoke Storage in Highland, Texas is no longer producing anything but Cool Aid, his trucks are detailed to pick up truckloads of cases from storage locations at nine different DOD storage locations.

POTUS SPEECH TO THE NATION

"Good evening, my fellow citizens of the United States. I come before you this day to address our concerns over the civil unrest we are seeing in the country related to the HVD virus epidemic. Although the virus is a real threat, it can be combated by the orderly implementation of vaccinations. The administration has seen conspiracy theories about the disease. Let me assure you that these broadcasts have grossly misrepresented the facts about the vaccines and have no basis in truth.

We are working diligently with the Department of Health and Human Services in an attempt to get the disease under control through the use of free vaccinations to all. The Army will begin to employ a program to provide free transportation to temporary military installations that are prepared to administer the protective vaccines. For this reason, we are having military locations set up near major cities across the United States, to deter the continued existence of unsecured lines at clinics.

Medical clinics and hospitals are now ordered to issue vaccinations only to those with verified appointments. This appointment protocol will decrease the need for long lines and improve inventory management by the medical providers.

Tomorrow at 9:00 A.M. Eastern Standard Time, there will be a website available to register appointments to be transported to receive your vaccines. The temporary military locations will be staffed with a great many more medical staff to provide shuttle service and administer the vaccinations to recipients in a safe manner. If you do not have access to a computer, you may make your appointments by calling 1-800-VACCINE. The name of the website is www.vaccineschedule.gov. We strongly suggest that you pre-schedule your appointments to expedite the process.

Both the phone number and website name will be on the banners of all television stations until it is determined that all people have received their vaccinations.

In addition to the concerns about the vaccines, it becomes necessary to control the current resultant civil disobedience.

This afternoon, I signed an executive order declaring a nationwide state of emergency to initiate a temporary state of martial law. The reason for this martial law is to combat the lawlessness being perpetrated on the streets of America, as criminals are taking advantage of the people who are simply attempting to get their vaccinations.

Also, I have signed a second order to set up temporary military locations and transportation to these locations for the administering of vaccinations.

Martial Law will begin tonight at Midnight. Until the order is rescinded, the military will impose a 6:00 PM to 6:00 AM curfew across the nation. Persons with jobs that conflict with this curfew will be required to receive a special permit to be carried on their person at all times outside the curfew hours.

We will also be implementing a voluntary gun buyback program immediately. This will help ensure that the military can do their jobs unimpeded. The buyback agents will provide proof of your ownership of all registered weapons which, will be returned to you once the martial law order is rescinded.

This message will be re-broadcast at the beginning of each hour for the next full week, for those who may have missed it today. I thank you for your commitment to the safety of all peoples within our borders. God Bless the United States of America."

At the bottom f the video:

Phone, "1-800-VACCINE"
Website, www.vaccineschedule.gov

* * *

Delphi's office

At the same time, Madam President is delivering her address to the nation, Chuck Delphi was on an anonymous phone call to Mr.D (Art Damone).

Delphi, "Mr. D – we have come to the point where it becomes necessary to decommission the commander in chief of the nation. I'm sure you've seen the news coverage lately. She is denying a conspiracy but she is a liar, I have recently received information linking her to the Chinese doctor from Bearlywoke. The only conspiracy here is the one where she is working with Beijing, China to facilitate a U.S. takeover."

Damone, "Why take her out – what about exposing her and going the legal route?"

Delphi, "Because the legal process takes much too long, she is responsible for tens of thousands of deaths each week. Impeachment would allow her to wipe out the population before her term ends."

Damone, "How do you want it done? I'm not into terrorism type of stuff with large numbers of collateral damage and a President is gonna cost you a lot."

Delphi, "Clean, Mr. D – it can look like Dr. Hampton if you want. I can provide something that works much faster, but getting close enough to her may be challenging."

Damone, "I will pick up the juice tomorrow – the same place as Hampton – 0300."

* * *

Whitehouse

At 0400, Art Damone is in the Whitehouse kitchen preparing the tray with fresh-squeezed orange juice and a blueberry bagel for the President. He had done work here before under other names and has his security clearances.

At 0500, during the President's shower, her juice and bagel were delivered. Art stepped into the bathroom reached through the shower putting his white-gloved hand across her mouth as he injected the chemical into the area between her legs that no M.E. would consider looking for injection marks. He didn't even need to add the chloral hydrate this time, she went down fast as the injection dispensed directly into the blood supply of the labia. A slight head trauma-impacted from a well-placed slam of her head on the tile and she was quietly placed on the floor of the shower. He left the water running. Her death appeared to be a fall.

He had no idea what this serum was, but it was good – better he believes than the stuff the Savior Unit is taking out of commission.

Forty minutes later, the first lady got up and found her wife in the shower. Five minutes later, Vice President Matthew Hominy was taking the oath of office as he became the new President of the United States.

Delphi and Carver debrief the new Vice President Hoge, by reminding him that the new POTUS is unaware of the DComm Group but considering that the public is currently revolting, against the HVD viral delivery. There will need to be a meeting of the DComm Group entities to regroup and consider how to handle the future of governing.

Free elections will cease to exist, so they have 10 months left with POTUS Hominy to try to get the uprising under control while the DComm Group focuses on the new rules.

The nationwide media reports indicate a tragic accident causing the death of President Talbot and babbled relentlessly, about the upcoming funeral proceedings. There were many condolences from other heads of state around the world, but consideration of their attendance was questionable. The United States was currently contagious and though there were assurances that there would be no risk of visiting world leaders being at risk, they felt they must respectfully decline to attend services. This slight was, of course grossly offensive to the widow/former First Lady, but graciously accepted by the current President Hominy, when considering the risk of the HVD epidemic.

VICE PRESIDENT ROBERT HOGE

(FORMER SECRETARY OF STATE)

Hoge feels like Stephanie Wolff has dropped the ball somehow, in allowing the Project Clearcut information to go public, so he would like to see her decommissioned or at least removed from her position. There was no absolute proof that the Project Clearcut Mission statement had been leaked but the rampant conspiracy theories seemed to indicate the possibility.

President Hominy had the constitutional right to appoint a new Vice President, but the sudden rise to the position of POTUS left him hopelessly unprepared for the position. Former President Talbot was a demonstrative person preferring to be in complete control of all things. VP Hominy had been a figurehead – nothing more.

When the staff of former President Talbot recommended Robert Hoge, the overwhelmed Hominy quickly conceded knowing there was little time before the elections and he would be overwhelmed with this epidemic coupled with a campaign. He was happy to let the supportive staff wash over him as he attempted to assume the role thrust upon him.

The New Vice President Robert Hoge meets with New President Hominy in the Situation Room.

Hoge, "Mr. President, I appreciate your appointment to this position. Unfortunately, we have attained these positions under such unfortunate circumstances, but we do have a country to run. I've recently been in meetings with Director Avery (CIA), Director Carver (FBI), and Acting Director Delphi (DOD). I'm sure you have been advised of the unrest in the country over the HVD virus epidemic. Former President Talbot's need to invoke martial law to try to maintain stability in the country was a necessary evil. But we have other concerns within the ranks of the government that are problematic."

Hominy, "Yes, I have been advised of the civilian population issues, what are your concerns within the ranks of the government?"

Hoge, "Well we have a Director of NSA, Stephanie Wolff. It appears that she has been abusing the power of her office and subsequently putting the national security at risk."

Hominy, "What has she done that rises to the level of national security concerns?"

Hoge, "It appears that she is involved with a conspiracy related to the HVD virus and possibly inciting the public insurrection that DOD and DHS are seeing."

Hominy, "Those are some pretty damning accusations. Do I need to get the DOJ involved to investigate her activity? Is her suspected activity worthy of impeachment or dismissal?"

Hoge, "Sir, investigations can take years. In the meantime, the country's security concerns mount. If it were any agency or position other than the head of NSA, of course, we would be suggesting an in-depth investigation.

But she is in a position with complete control of the national security. We do not believe that keeping her in the current position during a lengthy pending investigation would be prudent when considering her security access."

Hominy, "What would your team suggest then?"

Hoge, "We are suggesting that she should be dismissed or at least put on administrative leave and immediately remove her security clearance and access to NSA data until such time that she is indicted, convicted, or exonerated –to protect the country, Sir."

Hominy, "Is this in conflict with the 4th amendment regarding the due process?"

Hoge, "Of course she is entitled to due process, sir. We are just suggesting that for the security of the country, she should at least be denied access within NSA. We are not suggesting she should be denied due process. Of course, she could be reinstated if, after a thorough investigation, it was determined that she has done nothing wrong."

Hominy, "I see, of course, you are correct she should not have access to NSA records. I will see to this immediately, in the meantime, could you tell me who to speak with to advise me on the selecting and appointment of an Acting director?"

Hoge, "We will have a list of potential candidates for the position prepared for you within the hour, Sir."

The DComm Group had already selected her replacement options, but Hoge didn't want to seem presumptuous.

The President requested Stephanie's resignation which she already had waiting in addition to her two jets each of which was loaded to capacity with cargo. Both jets bore the cases labeled A and D. Both she and Chuck Delphi departed on these jets. Shortly after refueling in Hawaii, one of the jets disappeared suddenly over the South Pacific.

Rockwell has other generals in charge of different educational centers, recruiting the people to fight against the regime that is trying to destroy the government. The people are getting educated and leaving with materials to return to their cities and towns to educate others. This education is the motivation that will lead to an insurrection to destroy the DComm Group and take back the people's control of the government.

He has deployed all 50 states' National Guard with the mission to protect the people from the small groups tasked with martial law. Many of these were now getting educated about Project Clearcut and they are abandoning the Commander in Chief's orders to militarize the cities. The people have no desire to war against our military – they just want their freedom, liberty, and safety back, but like the revolution that began her independence – they would now fight to restore that which was being stripped away from them.

THE TRUCKERCADE

Long haul truck drivers do many things to stay awake on their cross country trips. They all leave at home their family and friends who may be at risk for the deadly HVD epidemic spreading across the states. Some of these drivers listen to music, some listen to their radios, but all talk to other drivers as they move products across the country. Many of these drivers, and also working commuters, listen to radio broadcasts to keep informed of what is going on in their cities and states with the HVD problem. So like the spreading virus, a few truck drivers who heard the CAPublican broadcast, quickly radio to other drivers what they had heard – about the virus being created and used as a weapon against the citizens.

The truckers call their families to warn them not to get immunizations, then share the news on their radios. But there is one unified response, it is the fury and they know where Bearlywoke is located.

Buddy Engles is one of these drivers. His wife Liz is a computer wiz. When he calls her and tells her what he just heard about the HVD, she tells him she had already heard about the breaking news on all the mainstream media television broadcasts. Buddy tells her, the truckers must do their part to stop this insanity and that she needs to find out where the immunizations are being distributed across the country. It took her an hour to get the information, but she was able to discover that nine distribution centers were sending the vaccines to city clinics and medical centers.

Buddy got the list and then HE went to work. As he made his way to Bearlywoke Storage in Highland Texas, his and other families used their radios to coordinate truckers near these hub distribution centers and set a plan in motion to make sure no vaccine was leaving those damn distribution warehouses. The truckers were blockading all nine of them! And every trucker was armed and prepared to defend these 'truckercades'.

The truckercades were met at the distribution centers by prepared and organized military contingents around the facilities. Doctor Trish Mason, Goose, and Beth McCallum arrived at Bearlywoke in a military helicopter which set down directly on top of the bed of a large Army transport truck situated in front of the security rod gate of Bearlywoke. Other heavily armed military vehicles were surrounding the interior perimeter of the campus.

Beth and Dr. Mason were outfitted with military protective gear while Goose had no protection, but had assured General Yabo, that, "`Goose has tools.`"

General Yabo, "Beth, are you sure you are up to this? And Dr. Mason?"

Both Dr. Mason and Beth gulped and nodded affirmative, the words didn't seem ready to leave their mouths.

Members of an Army security squad jumped out of another chopper as it landed inside the perimeter of the Bearlywoke campus. Their orders were to secure the area for the exit of the General and others.

General Yabo, speaking through a bullhorn, loudly demanded to know who was the person in charge of the truckercade situated at the main gate.

Buddy loudly responds, "The people of the United States are in charge, sir, but if you need a spokesman, I guess since I'm at the front of this line, that would be me!"

Through the bullhorn, Yabo now says, "Listen to me, I am General Yabolinski of the United States Army. WE are not the enemy of the people. WE are here to protect this facility because it is the only place where the HVD virus can be effectively and safely destroyed, to protect the country."

Buddy, "If the Army knows how to destroy it, why are our people dying from it? Some people are getting vaccinated and still DYING! There was a doctor on the news who said it is the vaccinations that are killing the people! So why the hell would the Army protect this place and those warehouses? My trucker friends tell me that those nine locations are surrounded by military protection too!"

Dr. Mason takes the bullhorn from the General. "I am Doctor Trish Mason, the person you heard on the CAPublican radio broadcast talking about the virus. Please listen to us. I am part of a small but growing team of people, patriots, who know the truth about the HVD and it is information that we are assembling to use to stop the genocide which was planned by a very small group of people within the government. This is NOT something that was planned by your government, but rather a small group intended to overthrow our government by committing genocide to reduce and control the population. Please listen to Beth McCallum, she is part of the Savior Unit who originally discovered the truth about the virus and have been working tirelessly to stop it." As she hands the bullhorn to Beth she quietly says, "Beth you can do this."

Beth opened her mouth to speak but found herself incapable of uttering a single word. Goose observed and assessed the situation, then reached for the American flag on the antenna of the transport. The MSA put the staff in

Beth's hands and said to the crowd of truckers, "I am MSA121068, medical assistant droid, Dr. Hampton killed for the creation of anti-virus, MSA was decommissioned to hide the truth about HVD, Beth and Joshua-human recommissioned MSA to save humanity, Truckers must now help Savior Unit save humanity. Listen to Beth-human now, she has tools of communication."

Goose puts a hand gently on Beth's arm, "Beth speaks for Goose" one blink.

Beth hands the flag to Goose as she takes the bullhorn and with the hand of Goose on her arm, she found her voice.

"The things that Dr. Mason, the General, and MSA Goose have said are true. There is a large story to tell about the small group of people we call the DComm Group intending to overthrow the government – but the most important thing you must know is that the Army is not your enemy. The Army has isolated all stores of the dangerous virus which needs to be transported to this facility where deep beneath the earth is equipment which can safely destroy the virus – this facility and those nine warehouses are not your enemies – the VIRUS is not your enemy.

Your true enemy is the fear and chaos created by a small group of oligarchs who have a plan to overthrow the government. Your true enemy is the division of people and the consuming fear and hatred of your fellow citizens. Even as I speak to you, now, President Hominy is acting to effect justice on the DComm Group of oligarchs. The true enemy remains, it is the enemy in each of us as we fear and distrust our neighbors. If we cannot learn to respect and trust each other, we will never be free of new groups with evil desires for power and control over us.

I implore you to help the Savior Unit, with your trucks and protection and trust, to bring the HVD material to this location for destruction, then to return to your homes and find a way to change your lives to protect your fellow citizens from the virus of distrust and hate!"

WHITEHOUSE SITUATION ROOM

President Matthew Hominy
Vice President Robert Hoge
General Alan Rockwell
General Hunter Yablonski (General Yabo)
Doctor. Emmett Rankin (reinstated CDC)
Travis Loki (acting Director FBI)
Doctor Jill Rider (HHS)
Doctor Joanna Moore
Joshua Klein
MSA 121068

General Rockwell meets with President Hominy bringing proof of the Project Clearcut, the DComm Group including tapes of discussions and plans for the assassination of President Talbot, and the final straw, the proof of the recycling of bodies. Rockwell recommends General Hunter Yablonski to replace Delphi as Director of DOD and to shut down the body recycling project (homeless shelter food). President Hominy orders that the DOJ arrest Delphi immediately to hold until a grand jury hearing may be convened.

The President views presentations by Emmett Rankin, Joanna Moore, MSA, and Joshua Klein advising him of the details of the efforts to neutralize the dissemination of the virus across the nation. He approves of the measures and assures them that they will have the full support and cooperation of the military to continue to collect and destroy all live virus material.

He then asks General Yabo for his report on what is being done with the bodies. General Hunter Yablonski, explains that under his direction, all recycling efforts have ceased and personnel involved in the effort have been detained until such time that a full inquiry is done to ascertain culpability in the activity that has been taking place. As to the deceased; most have no way to identify family, so General Yabo recommends it is probably best to cremate the bodies. It could be represented to the people as a public health concern because the deceased died of the deadly virus – as such, the safety of the masses must be considered. General Yabo assures the President that every possible means to identify bodies will be employed, to allow notification of family where there is information available.

President Hominy asks Jill Rider (HHS) what the status is on the virus that reached the medical facilities. Jill tells President Hominy that she has issued an immediate mandatory stoppage of all HVD serums and the quarantine of all serum within medical facilities. There will need to be teams of people to remove all AVBW# serums in medical facilities.

General Rockwell assures the President that the nine storage distribution centers identified by the Savior Unit have been, and remain, blockaded by the Army and volunteer contingents of armed civilian truck drivers. With the President's permission, he will order the transport and destruction of the truckloads of HVD inventory.

UNIFICATION

As the government sought to impose justice against the DComm Group, what might have resulted in an insurrection now became a time to heal. Rather than fight against the government, the people began to formulate a path to peace as they sought to heal the division, hate, and mistrust. The truckercades assisted in organized transportation of the serums to Bearlywoke to be destroyed in the secure incinerators deep in the recesses of the building.

The healing began in churches and arenas where speakers went, some to preach, some to simply motivate the people to help the helpless and give of themselves whatever assistance they had to offer. The country hadn't reached the current state of division and chaos overnight and healing would take time, but the people were taking small steps to a better life.

The war was now against chaos and distrust and the victory would be a unified nation.

EPILOG

The United States lost over 12 million people to the HVD virus. But the remaining had a newfound respect for a constitutional republic of governance in the United States. Gone was the vitriolic partisanship as the awareness of government by and for the people, surpassed the allegiance to a political party. The country had made some serious mistakes in believing that a handful of government entities could manage all aspects of people's lives.

The people learned that the only way to prevent lawlessness was to return to the law as written by the founders.

Dave Tillis is currently Acting Director of the NSA.

Beau Clark will never get that date with the beautiful Stephanie Wolff.

Joanna continues as Director at Bearlywoke, manufacturing and packaging AV_JMV2030, the anti-virus vaccine. This action is taken in the unlikely event that there is a cache of HVD virus serum that has not been destroyed.

Cool Man now works as Deputy Director of Bearlywoke Storage and is, well, cool.

MSA121068 (Goose), Joshua Klein, and Beth McCallum work for Bearlywoke reconciling stores of HVD. Discovering that records have been altered precipitates the need for a massive audit and investigation of Bearlywoke inventory records.

Adrian Mouse takes early retirement so she and her partner can share the task of being caregivers to her friend Dave Foote.

General Rockwell is appointed to the position of Chief Advisor to the President.

General Hunter Yablonski is appointed to Acting Director Department of Defense.

President Matthew Hominy is busily working on his campaign for the Presidency and attempting to assure the population that the HVD conspiracy has been contained and the perpetrators are awaiting their consequences which will be executed to the fullest extent of the law.

Drew Legend continues as Director of Homeland Security.

Jill Rider continues the public media blitz to reassure the public that the HVD epidemic is controlled.

Darla Avery continues as Director of the CIA – her participation in the DComm Group process, as well as that of Vice President Robert Hoge's, are as of yet undiscovered.

The USA voter population is working hard scrutinizing

their voting choices for the upcoming elections – there will no longer be party-line voters as there is a nationwide determination to replace the old guard politicians with candidates who have demonstrated commitment to the constitution.

In custody, awaiting, or fugitive from charges ranging from abuse of power, domestic terrorism, and other criminal acts including treason: Michael Carver (former director FBI).

Missing but with equal charges on the FBI's and Interpol's most wanted lists:

> Chuck Delphi (former DOD)
> Stephanie Wolff (former NSA)
> Dr. Yīshēng Swáng (former Director Bearlywoke) now the number one on both the FBI's and Interpol's most-wanted lists.

Art Damone is on his way to Beijing, China – this will not be a vacation, but his vendetta. Art has now gone rogue, he is the Black Op Patriot. He is accompanied by MSA1201068 – affectionately nicknamed Goose. Stay tuned...

A NOTE TO MY READERS ABOUT THE DECOMMISSIONED TRILOGY

The prophetic behavior of the fictional virus in the Decommissioned trilogy has not been edited to reflect the behavior of the 2020 Covid-19 Novel Corona Virus.

At the time Decommissioned was written, in late 2017, there was no real-world Covid-19 pandemic. Though the Decommissioned Trilogy is about a fictional virus, it is different in some ways, from the present worldwide pandemic. The similarities, parallels, and possibilities continue to be staggering......

OTHER BOOKS BY MARYELLEN HUNTER

<u>DECOMMISSIONED</u>

Book one in the Decommissioned trilogy and the prequel to SAVIOR UNIT.

In Decommissioned Josh and Beth stumble upon the partially decommissioned Medical Services Android (later affectionately named "Goose" – as in golden goose) and work to recommission it. In the process they discover its mission: "MUST SAVE MANKIND" and the reason behind it.

Hunted by the FBI they encounter other individuals who are also discovering the truth to the increasing number of deaths related to a vaccine. As these individual heroes coalesce, the SAVIOR UNIT is formed. Their mission will be to expose the truth and the perpetrators and stop the genocide being wrought on the citizens of the United States.

DECOMMISSIONED CHINA

Coming in 2021 Decommissioned China is the third in the Decommissioned Trilogy. In Decommissioned China key members of the DComm Group move to Asia and continue their genocidal effort to effect a new world order. Art Damone follows them and…

IOTAA
(to be published by Fulton Books 2021)

IOTAA is a story of survival, corruption, greed, adversity, adventure, intrigue, competition, and fantasy – wrapped up and tied with a bow of irony.

IOTAA is a story that will never be forgotten!

ZORBECK

A fictional thriller to be on the market early in 2021. Zorbeck arrives on planet Earth by accident. Its feeding process provides its amorphic ability to recreate more of its kind which must be hunted and destroyed before its food supply is exhausted.

ABOUT THE AUTHOR

Maryellen grew up in Toledo Ohio in the 1940s. Reading was a lifetime of books and stories. As early as her elementary school days there were Encyclopedias with their youth books filled with tales from Huckleberry Finn to Little Women. Every Saturday morning, she made the trek to the local library to borrow the maximum number of books allowed. Near the library was a nursing home, so this weekly trip was a double-duty trip of visiting the elderly of the facility. Reading to the residents, singing songs with and for them, and listening to their tales of their own life experiences was a joy to her.

She was inspired by the thrilling stories by Edgar Allan Poe. The Mask of the Red Death and Telltale Heart were stories to be read many times and still sixty years later hold a special place on the bookshelf. Her love of poetry compelled her to memorize Poe's The Raven and William Ernest Henley's Invictus.

Throughout all the reading, she wrote volumes of letters and prose with no thought of publishing any of them, it was just important to put words on paper.

Her writing style is uniquely designed to allow her audience to envision each character within their imaginations. She creates diversity within her heroes and villains and strives to provide the opportunity for you to share your perceptions of each character.

Facebook:

https://www.facebook.com/maryellen.hunter.1690

https://www.facebook.com/Maryellen-Hunter-Author-Page-106094434607982